The Rescuer's Path

SECOND EDITION

Paula Friedman

The Rescuer's Path

SECOND EDITION

Paula Friedman

Plain View Press, LLC  www.plainviewpress.net
1101 W 34th Street, Suite 404 Austin, TX 78705

ISBN: 978-1-63210-045-0
Second Edition, 2018, published by Plain View Press
First edition: 978-1-935514-88-6
Library of Congress Control Number: 2011930980

Cover photo *Tree Lake* by the author
Cover design by Pam Knight
Title-page art *Remembrance* by the author
Author photograph by Cathy Friedman

To Tom, Roberto, Pamela,
and the others in the struggle

and

To Chris and Joseph

Contents

Malca, 2008

Back then? I was still differentiating.

This is the beginning, I would think, bounding down the stairs to the blare of "Let It Be" from my sister's stereo, racing out past the big forsythia, and heading downhill toward the "L" bus, always wondering how I ought to live and what to study when I got to college—meanwhile, every day discovering new styles (those black fringed jeans Mom despised!) and my own views on ethics and the war. Sometimes I would wonder what it must be like for people old and poor, for someone being bombed in Vietnam, for alien creatures on some other world, but mostly I read and studied—an awkward, sheltered teen with no idea how to be popular or what to say to boys. Full of myself, but fortunately curious.

"I am someone who must become strong," I told my best friend Nina, smoking grass for the first time in her parents' recreation room, "but stay open to people, to the world. To possibility." The rest, I knew only in theory—adventures, procedures, how we ever reached this place, what can be lost. Life was ahead, if I dared—the beginning of everything.

I had no idea what lay out there.

Part 1. Off-Trail

(Summer 1971)

Malca

It was coming into the full moon, that early summer evening—blistering heat after too cold a winter, antiwar protests downtown near the White House, rumors of another murder in Bethesda—when young Malca Bernovski turned the stallion for the first time toward a red-clay gully at the northern edge of Rock Creek Park.

Ears back, Dragon reared; legs stiff, he fought his tiny trainer. She let him plunge, her long hair flopping, and struggled to stay balanced. Urging him sharply forward, she sat bolt upright as she'd seen the stable manager, Gerilee, do a hundred times and, hands gentle but steady on the reins, guided him along an overgrown game trail into the steep gully, down between high banks. The horse no longer balked; he was nearly to the bottom, almost to the water—indeed, his left foreleg had already stepped into the turgid current—when he glanced to his left and once more reared.

"Stop it!" Nearly thrown, Malca flung herself against the gleaming neck. "Down—there's nothing scary here." But at that moment she saw the form.

Black hair grimed by mud and water, covered with dirt and blood, a man lay half-hidden behind the vines and granite rocks. He barely seemed to breathe. Blood was caked along his torn, green-and-blue striped sleeves and down across one thigh, his hands spread flat against the clay, his legs lay helpless in the shallow current. Shivering, badly injured—but no one ever came here, and this man was haggard, filthy. He must be someone desperate—crazy maybe, even the Bethesda murderer. Her eyes caught the pallor under the olive skin, the foreign hollowness of the narrow cheeks. Could be that bomber who'd blown up the soldiers, downtown.

The horse rose higher, kicking out. The man moaned, frightened or in pain. Whoever he was, he couldn't move and he didn't look much bigger than she was. Eyes fixed on his face, she jerked the reins so Dragon's forelegs landed to one side.

"Whoa." Her voice stayed firm; only her body trembled. "It's okay, I'm here." But she should turn the horse's head right now and flee—for once remember her mother's warning, *It's too risky for a girl, out in those woods.*

With a sighing sound, the man turned his eyes and looked up. It seemed difficult for him. Black eyes, intelligent.

A cool breeze stirred the oaks. Dragon snorted. Leaning her weight onto one hand, Malca swung her right leg over the saddle.

The man kept trying to focus on her. He must be twenty-two, even older. *You've more brains than this,* she told herself, hopping to the ground. And it was time to get back to the stable. Gripping the reins, she squatted down. "Can you talk?"

The pale lips barely opened. She only caught a word like "so" or "don't." But when she started to lean closer, her hair nearly touched that filthy body. "Can't you say what's wrong?" She hesitated. "I better go get someone to come help."

Flinging up a hand, the man jerked; a sort of spasm shook his chest and head.

"Someone who can help you," she said.

His blood was spreading on the ground; his hands clawed at the earth. The afternoon that the Haradays' cat had got hit by a truck and she had tried to save it, it had clawed and clawed in that same way.

"All right. All right, I won't go. You can stay here." She didn't mean it as a promise.

The eyes searched for her, maybe gratefully. Then they closed. A black fly buzzed across his face—as if he had just died.

She lurched toward Dragon. Petting the thick mane, she watched the man's prone figure, strained to see his chest move. Then she heard a harsh, rasping sound as he took a breath.

Only, how could she keep someone breathing? He was doing okay, though, staccato but a regular rhythm—no need to touch the grimy chest. Just check for bleeding and . . . She couldn't remember the rest. Along his left arm, under the twisted shreds of sleeve, a blotchy area surrounded a deep round hole—like pictures of a bullet wound. It looked so real.

"This has got to be cleaned." She mustn't let him see that she was scared. "Let's get you on dry land, first." Forcing herself to grab the sticky shoulders, she tried to pull him up the bank. It was almost impossible, though, and when she slipped and let go, he groaned, a sound he stifled but that made her want to hide. Leaning against the red-clay slope, she braced her feet against the trunk of an ancient forsythia and began, slowly to not hurt him, to drag him from the creek.

"Okay," she breathed at last. "Okay."

For the clay shelf here, though rough, seemed nearly dry; an almost solid line of brush and vines and one high boulder screened him from the path, and the overhanging bank gave a bit of shelter. But those gaping wounds had to be cleaned, and that meant touching him again—and he stank, not only with sweat. He could be somebody deadly, in spite of those eyes. Again she took a step back toward the horse.

Long ago, someone in Europe had rescued Mom and Granma; some things, one just did. Patting Dragon, she jerked open the saddlepack, pulled out the emergency kit that Gerilee made every horse trainer carry. She turned. "Wake up," she urged the man. "Please."

His eyes opened. "Go on, miss." Nearly too weak to hear, his voice was polite, precise.

HE DID NOT CRY OUT WHEN SHE WASHED THE WOUNDS AND PUT ON THE iodine and covered them with gauze—the bullet hole or whatever it was, and that raw mess along the outside of one thigh, skin mixed with blood and shreds torn from his jeans. His skeletal face just stared, with an empty look that wasn't only pain. And when she asked him to turn his left arm so she could clean the wound there, he was too weak. He kept on shivering, so she untied her windbreaker from behind the saddle and stretched it across him. Then she remembered her wool scarf—Mom was always bugging her, "Carry something warm, dear, just in case."

As she lifted the scarf from the pack, Dragon whinnied. Past the thick trees, it was growing dark; people would be getting upset, back at the stable. She stroked the horse's muzzle. If they came looking for her, they would find this person. He must be a fugitive of some kind, the way he'd panicked—maybe not a murderer, or even the People's Liberating whatever-it-was bomber, but someone in hiding. Maybe a draft dodger—he was no foreigner, from his voice. "I need to go soon," she said.

But if she left, he could die.

His lips, so pale they looked white, moved in a half-twitch. His words—which might have been "And so?" but sounded more like "absurd"—were followed by a choking sigh. It made her want to pat him, to show him he'd soon be strong again.

"I have to take the horse back now," she said. "Otherwise they'll come searching." She wasn't sure he understood. "Here"—she pulled the windbreaker tight around him, wrapping the scarf so it covered the back of his head—"stay warm." She placed the half-full canteen beside his right hand, along with a box of crackers, the only food in her saddlebag. Pulling off his waterlogged shoes and socks, she covered his feet with her new issue of *Horse & Saddle* and a pile of crinkled leaves. He had stopped shivering, but what if the night turned cold?

"My Mom will be picking me up," she said. "She may be at the stable already, she gets frantic fast. I'll come back tomorrow. If I can." She didn't know what else to say. "No, I will." He just kept staring, eyes glittery.

Hurriedly, she untied Dragon's reins. Like someone crossing slippery ice, she started to back up, caught now by that stare that seemed to follow her—until, beyond the shrubbery, she turned and led the stallion up the gully path.

For the first time since she'd climbed down from the saddle, fear took over; it almost made her wet her pants. The game path was already dark, and oaks and maples crowded close, though the sky still glowed with light. Dragon pranced, ears stiff, prepared to bolt if she tried to mount. The bomber, people said, was insane—and dangerous crazy people lurking in the park's thick woods had been her parents' biggest argument against the riding job.

GERILEE CAME MARCHING FROM THE STABLE OFFICE. "HEY, A *JOB* MEANS getting back on time, lady. And paying attention where you ride. You pull this again, no more Dragon-light for you here. Get it?"

Malca nodded, head bowed, clasping the damp reins tightly and shaking in her wet clothes. It had been a sudden inspiration—ride Dragon into Rock Creek, slide off, pretend she was late because she'd been too busy looking at the rising moon and fallen in. No, a dumb idea—Gerilee had trusted her.

"And that five-dollar emergency kit? You couldn't remember to strap shut your saddlepack?" The stable manager's deep voice laughed, but her eyes were hard. She tossed a mended bridle up over the doorframe, pulling stiffly on its cheekstrap. "I mean, you know better, damn it." Again she laughed. "Never mind—this once, we'll let it go. I guess we all fall off sometime. But only once, Malca—you all right on that?"

It was the same thing Gerilee had said back in May, hiring her to exercise the stallion. "Let him race himself out to his heart's content—you all right on that? That's a mustang, you know, a rebel like me." They had been soaping saddles in the tackroom, under the horseshow trophies and the psychedelic poster of a dove with giant claws. "You run that horse three times a week—more, if you work out. And you will; you're not the timid little crybaby folks think." Now, slouched against the wall, Gerilee finally smiled. "Remember when you were half the size of all the other little squirts and you'd tumble off of every horse we tried? Even Layover?"

Malca nodded. She remembered, and how much it had mattered—horses, riding, all that. "Even Misty." She smiled back. Glad to, glad to be here. Here in this moment, here in the warm. In reality. With the stable manager and Dragon—and even Mom, who was coming slowly toward them, stepping awkwardly across the littered yard in her "downtown" office shoes and narrow skirt.

To be here—not worrying about that person, who could be very dangerous.

Who might be dead by tomorrow. What if she went back to find crows eating those eyes?

"Mom, I need to get home." She struggled to keep her voice low, to speak the way somebody college-bound, someone without secrets, would. "Mom, let's get home fast so I can dry off. And tomorrow I'll ride Dragon really carefully." She turned to Gerilee. "If I may? I'll do it extra."

Gerilee tossed her dark curls, standing proud the way she must have in her Freedom Rider days. "I don't know why not, Malca. We want to see you succeed."

"Indeed." Her mom, lighting a cigarette, breathed out smoke. "Actually, Miss Tassevara, I am very happy for this chance to thank you.

This is the first interest Malca has stuck with, since when." The smile was fake. "Whenever," Mom corrected herself.

The stable manager's eyes went wide. Gerilee knew about horses and teaching riding, but she didn't understand Mom, what Mom had gone through back in Europe, how fast she got upset. Gerilee was saying, "She seems a pretty on-top kid to me, Mrs. Bernovski. She's got"—stressing the word—"smarts."

Mom must be furious; she just blew a second long puff from her nose. "Brains, yes. But when it comes to persidurance"—it was embarrassing, Mom still mixed up words—"not so much. Mind may be enough, back in Poland or someplace. But not here."

"That so?" The stable manager was putting on a client-helping smile. "That little girl used to sit around and scarcely say 'Boo,' when she didn't go running home crying, and now she's into every nook and cranny. You know she's got all our trails by heart?"

But Gerilee couldn't see that Mom was hurting. Though it wasn't clear what got to Mom; sometimes she acted totally alone.

Like that man in the woods, who'd maybe said "absurd." He needed help, but he had clawed the ground like the Haradays' cat to get away.

Gavin

No, screw it, screw it. That was back then, no different from the nights he'd worked the Mall, but here was now. Not only what he'd done but what he would have done. No difference, not with what would happen— soon, tonight, next moment.

Bare words—except this shaking, blood strewn over everywhere as if he were some sacrificial animal. If he instead had left and climbed up to the avenue . . . He hadn't.

Evidently. Given what was coming, not to waste time on the obvious. Think, rather, on the logic. The logic of infinities was that there could not be a logic. Yet what the joke about infinity had been, he didn't remember. Or how his clothes had got so wet. This must be wrong, even if he were required to join the count.

For no more war, ring the tambourines / clanging for to thunder you home—

Yet screw that stuff, for real. Jennie once brought a purple balloon, the first day of his trial. Each one—Jennie, Maura, Jason, Sal—had been a universe, thus infinite, alive and thus uncountable. A core in each, who loved, absurdly mobius. Together they had crawled in from the Hamer Woods, through mud thicker than this, in heavy rain—brave Sallie, Maura with her red hair dripping—but he on point, the one with skills to clear the circuits, find a route across the fence, and inside start dismantling operations.

Now he'd never . . . Forget it. Not to waste the grace of these few moments of lucidity. *For peace clangs no more crystal / where the rivers sang to—*

Skip songs, songs conveyed nothing; moments conveyed. Life conveyed. This body—not him, couldn't be—jerked like a punctured balloon in repetitious struggling to escape.

He must.

Across the glade in blaring sunlight stood a girl of long straight hair, a primal actuality, who pricked her ears and said, "I'll tell, and they will know." Who knew and said, "You caused death—have a taste."

He tried to laugh, mind still attuned to numbers' rhythms, but the sun heaved from the stinky mud, jabbed light through leaves overhead to prove that hope, too, joked, and Time itself reversed; the bombed-out Earth spun backward over his wounds.

Death cures the clay, / life furls its way—

Damn songs—nothing else. Nothing. Outside the logic, there was choice or chance. The problem with the blue light *and* the pills had been, when one looked carefully, a matter of unless sufficient empathy—

And then, he had—

Now his fingers could grasp nothing. A jacket, fallen on him, made things warmer.

Malca

At least the night had not been cold. But morning was thick with miasmic heat as she rode the bus to Chevy Chase and then another down the Beltway to the road beside the stables. Stashing the shopping bag near Upper Meadow, she rested briefly, swatting at mosquitoes. The bag held a blanket and her poncho from riding camp, first-aid supplies, scissors, water—all she could carry—and penicillin from her mother's downstairs "just-in-case" drawer.

Walking toward the stable, she pulled change from the pocket of her bell-bottoms—enough for the bus home. Gerilee paid summer help only once a month. In the white-shingled barn, all the horses were in their stalls except Misty and two mares. The stable manager was out—"teaching the littles," said Eric, the old groom who drank too much but kept good track of everyone. Dragon fought when she tried to saddle him so she had to ask Eric's help; he could calm any horse or frightened child.

"Smart little stud," he commented, clamping the saddle tight while she climbed to Dragon's back. "Way too hot a day for getting ridden."

She smiled and started off at a brisk walk. Soon, striking the path to Upper Meadow, she gathered her supplies, then forced the horse into a canter. An oriole soared from the grass. Stifling hot here, but she needed to hurry; she must help that person—if he still was alive.

Two miles farther on, she curved from Western Trail onto the overgrown game path and, Dragon finding his own careful footing, squeezed down toward the gully. Everything was silent; vines on the clay banks hung in the windless air. She leaned far forward in the saddle, searching. There were the screening bushes, the dark overhang with its shielding vines, that heap of rocks, the largest like a boulder. And, beyond, the man—lying exactly as she had left him, her windbreaker to his chin, scarf loose about his head, canteen untouched beside him though his lips looked cracked and dry. But still alive—she made out his chest moving. The black eyes might even see her, though she couldn't tell. What must the night have been for him?

Afraid Dragon would bolt, she lashed the reins around a dogwood. She dragged down the supplies, dodging a kick, and left the horse to nibble at waterside plants. The man's wounds didn't seem much better—maybe a bit less red. She thought again of Sonja hiding people in her attic, daring to help someone no matter what. Kneeling, she lifted the jacket and began to wash the man, finding courage finally to cut away his clothes and clean the filth off his skin. The odor nauseated her, though, and afterward she sat on a rock upstream, taking long breaths. But he was shivering again, so she quickly dressed his wounds and spread the blanket over his chest. Then she fit a straw into a juice can and, helping him raise his head, placed the other end to his lips. He only sighed, as if unable to try anymore.

"Come on," she urged, "of course you can." A drop or two ran into his mouth, and she heard him swallow. He took three more swallows before his head rolled back against her arm.

"Well, that's all right." It was as if he were Dragon—or her little sister, Hannah, when very young. She wanted him to be all right, to get better. He was sleeping.

A mockingbird started up nearby. She listened, but no one came near. Dragon stared resignedly into space, only snorting at an occasional small animal—a squirrel or frog—in the brush. An hour passed, maybe two. She sat still, trying to recognize bird calls, holding this stranger against her aching upper arm and giving warmth that might save his life.

About three o'clock, a shaft of sun came directly through the trees onto his eyelids, and they opened. She started. The eyes looked darker—softer, more alive.

"You held me?" His voice was again precise. She squeezed his arm, to say *You'll be all right*, but his lips moved and he asked, though barely audibly, "This whole time?"

He must be confused. "Just this afternoon." Again she added, "You do need a doctor, you know. Bullets have to come out."

He didn't act frantic this time, only sad. "They went through," he breathed, as if at something silly. "Through *me*."

IT WAS LATE THE NEXT AFTERNOON BEFORE SHE COULD GET BACK TO Park Northern Stables. She rode into the gully to find the man unconscious, and it was only by coaxing juice and water from a straw into his mouth—until he would convulsively, and as if unwillingly and from a far distance, swallow—that she could get liquids into him at all.

The next day, she told her parents she was spending the afternoon with her friend Nina, whom they trusted. Traveling on foot from the bus stop, staying far from the stable to avoid being sighted, she came again to the gully and sat for another two hours, sometimes humming a song the way Mom used to when she or Hannah was sick, beside the silent form that seemed to hover halfway out of life.

AT THE BREAKFAST TABLE THE NEXT MORNING, HER MOTHER WAS suspicious when Malca said, "I'm going downtown today, to the National."

"Why is that, dear?" The words came around a cigarette.

"To the National *Gallery*. Why do you think?" Mom's probing could get extreme, but it felt horrid to lie. And hard to concentrate, except on whether to risk carrying the big shoulder-bag with that pair of Dad's old workpants from the basement. Very old—probably from his field-research days with NASA.

"I didn't know you were 'into' art." Mom put a Mendelssohn recording on the stereo and started revving up the sarcasm. "Perhaps you will come to the Frick sometime when I am curating. Or this is something new from Nina? I hadn't heard."

Why should it matter who something came from? "There's lots," Malca snapped, "you haven't heard." But that was too true. She cut an orange into wedges and lifted two slices of bread from the toaster.

Her mother lit another cigarette. "Have it your way, Malki."

"Mom, you want some toast?" She held out hers; she had scarcely begun to butter it. She hated it when Mom looked at her patiently this way, like waiting for disaster.

Two hours later, when finally she reached the gully, the man was no better. Though he seemed to hear when she tried to sing—a lullaby, then "Kumbayah"—and drank on his own after she put the straw between his lips, he made no sound when she cleaned the wounds, and he didn't seem to see anything, the few times his eyes opened, at all.

That night, she couldn't read *The Speculative Philosophers* or even the Farina novel, but kept starting to run downstairs to say to Mom, "It's because somebody hid you and Granma from the Nazis." Dad would agree, "She's got a point there, Beyla," and they'd all get in the car and bring the person home, into the safe, dry house.

But no, this was thinking like a child; what Mom would do instead was get cold furious and snap "You make comparisons?" and look a hundred years old. And Dad would call the police, and later, half-joking the way he did, say, "This isn't one of your little stray kittens or injured robins, Bubbie. What you need is a bit of horse sense." There would be sirens, men racing into the gully with guns.

Only, without help, a person hurt so bad could die. Even this moment. Pushing up from her desk so fast she banged her knee, she ran to the window, pressed her nose against the damp screen. Only four blocks to Connecticut Avenue, but the Beltway Express didn't run after ten at night. In the pink darkness, rain drizzled steadily.

SHE SMILED SO HARD SHE COULD FEEL IT, THE CORNERS OF HER MOUTH pushing up her cheeks, to see him glance up quickly, hearing her and Dragon. He half-leaned on an elbow on the blanket, a juice container empty at his side. He was watching her with a terribly intelligent look.

Seeing her windbreaker draped across those dirty shoulders, she felt her stomach lurch with fright. But this man could barely move. Unless by now he was just faking; it was five days since she'd found him. On the news, they said a suspect had been caught in the Bethesda murders but the bomber remained loose and dangerous. He had fled into the woods . . . But that had happened miles from here, down where the park road went under Calvert Bridge.

"Who are you?" she started to ask, but he spoke first.

"Why are you helping me?" His voice was hard to hear.

"Because"—she said the first thing she thought—"you're hurt."

"You're . . ." A sort of tremor went over him, and the weakness sucked him down so he fell back to lie flat on the blanket.

"I'm what?"

He just lay there. Finally he said, "You're not afraid?"

She didn't answer. They said the bomber belonged to some little-known group called People's Liberation Tribe, and was not only dangerous but insane.

"Does your, does your"—it took him a minute to finish, as if he'd forgotten something—"your mother know you're here?" He seemed to smile or something, but not at her. Maybe he was just glad someone was there. But it made no sense. Too quickly, she washed his wounds and placed the gauze and iodine at his side, shoving the penicillin bottle closer. "To stop infection," she said. She felt embarrassed, scaring so easily—it was part of what she had to change. "You take those pills."

He didn't answer, just stared. Everything was where he could reach it himself, but really she wasn't sure he was strong enough.

ON THE TELEVISION NEWS, THE FBI MAN SAID, "WE HAVE NEW EVIDENCE linking the Flag Day truck-bomber"—or some phrase like that—"with the so-called peace activist convicted two years ago of destroying federal property at Port Ruh Naval Base. Even worse was planned, according to federal prosecuters at that time. We cannot divulge details."

"Oh yes, police with their secret evidence." Mom's eyes blinked fast. She sat on one end of the couch, next to her ashtray; smoke puffed between the words. "Governments."

"Beyla, the girls don't need to hear all this." Dad had been getting comfortable in his wing chair, under the enameled wall clock that had once been Granma's, research journals stacked up by his feet. "They can draw their own conclusions. Besides, little pitchers tend to spill whatever drops into their ears."

"Hanna and Malki aren't so little." Then Mom went silent. The news was showing Vietnamese peasants being marched away somewhere, hands tied behind their backs.

"Should I turn it off?" Dad got to his feet. Squinting, Mom snatched up her cigarettes. *Don't you girls ever say one word,* Dad had warned once, *when your mother gets like that.*

"Just sit—just sit, Daniel." Mom still seemed calm, but in a moment she would shrink back in the chair, the way she did when she got *like that*, criticizing everything, and begin to cry. But never mind—it wasn't Mom's old-Europe memories that were important now, it was her point about secret evidence: anything the FBI told the news could just be lies.

The picture on the screen had been fuzzy, someone thin and young. He might not be the person out there in the gully.

IT WAS NOT THAT SHE HAD TO LISTEN, OVER ROAST CHICKEN DINNER AT Dad's sister's house, to Mom complaining how the vacuum cleaner kept acting up and Aunt Ellen saying "Everything's such a *drama* for you, Beyla," while Dad pretended not to laugh and Mom's lips puffed in and out around a cigarette. It was not even that Mom and Dad both loved her but they'd never help.

It was the way that, leading Dragon this afternoon from the gully up the red clay path, she'd felt she was walking out into an unreal world.

The maroon paint of Aunt Ellen's dining room was like that clay, blood-colored with no way out. Maybe songs could not get through what that man must be caught in—not only pain or bullets but something else, maybe something he'd done or something else that made him stare into the sky and not try to get well. She should have sung him the other song, the Aaron one. All through her chicken wings and Aunt Ellen's salade niçoise, she kept thinking about that song.

"Aaron was a scholar but he turned into a hero, he was brave," Granma used to say. Granma's apartment, over the courtyard on Connecticut, had been full of tiny porcelain figurines and heavy quilts. "The Nazis made us walk through snow until our feet froze," Granma told them, once. Aaron had been Granma's son, Mom's big blond brother. "When the people told the fighters to go out into the forests," Granma would say, "my Aaron said, 'But no, we'll stay and fight beside you in the ghetto.' Oh, I told him I could fight too, I said I am not too old, but he said, 'Ma, since you and Beyla have a chance, you take it.' So when the troops came—already it was Passover—your *mamaleh* and I were hiding with my Pole. Eight months, until they found us. But years later, once a woman came to Washington and told me how my Aaron had died fighting and so brave." Then Granma would sing the fighters' song.

"Daniel, she's giving the children nightmares," Mom had said, one evening, standing between the bushes by their front screen door. "It's over, can't she leave him any peace?" And Dad had answered, "Aaron-the-brave," but very gently, like the world's softest words. Now, watching Mom and Dad and Aunt Ellen squabble across the dinner table, Malca wondered if Uncle Aaron would have been like them. Probably. But of course if he and Granpa Chaim had lived, everything would be different and she herself might not even exist—which definitely had to do with meaning and non-meaning, though it was hard to think with Mom complaining on and on about Dad's parents' "snobbing my accent again, this Pesach," and Aunt Ellen telling Hannah, "Dear, you are very smart—now aren't you smart? I'm sure it can't be *that* impossible to find a decent lipstick for a pretty girl your age."

And none of it was real—not with that person out there, desperate. Desperate just as Granma and Aaron and Mom had been, and families right this minute in Vietnam. Aunt Ellen brought a tray of raspberry muffins from the kitchen for dessert, and Malca took one, lifting it carefully on its yellow paper napkin.

If only she had sung that person in the gully the song.

Gavin

The music first would bring the new considerations of what must be done. And, split infinity, he'd tried. So that perhaps today he had the right to ask to simply end, in spite of what he once had done or left undone—could argue that the process took too long. A grieving man would say, "So you like logic jokes?" He, however, woke and laughed—for anyone of lost lucidity must either laugh or count, or cease to count, within the total, but instead he had crept here.

Yeah, and you were the one who claimed he'd go discover galaxies, remember? And incidentally write the music of your time.

His head at least could turn now, but thus a wind sprang up; another set-up, obviously. That girl again—straight brows, small form, the simple shirt and jeans of money. Coming closer, saying "I'm so sorry." A rich man's daughter, playing at first aid.

Yet this was the girl who'd stood inside the night. He had to show her she must let the music flow. She kept asking, "Why?" and trying—he had not understood—to save. To save him.

Malca

Wind rushed through the woods—a thunderstorm approaching. The canvas she had stretched above the man, and camouflaged with leaves and vines, could easily fall, strung between two branches and a narrow root that twisted from the overhang.

Better watch out for yourself first—the thought sounded like her parents; only, now she knew.

Gavin—that was the name on the news photos, Gavin Hareen. The fugitive confirmed by the new witness as the person skulking, nine days ago, in the brush just after the explosion. The bomber who had fled, wounded, into the park. They would catch him soon, the chief had promised. The news showed other photos of him, too—one of a smiling boy around Hannah's age, and one hard to make out but familiar, a man with empty eyes.

She did not understand—now what most frightened her was the danger to him. *Maybe this is how a killer strikes; he seems helpless and you start to like him, and then—wham.*

But as she rode around the curve and saw his broken form, fear seemed absurd. He could barely sit up—able to pull himself along the ground but mostly just waiting, patient and still.

Lately, so much was absurd, and not just what people said about life. Making war on a tiny country was absurd, and her parents acting as if they never disagreed, and Eric arguing she had to bring in Dragon earlier. What she wanted was to live in honesty and truth. As did this person, apparently—haunted, somehow, but struggling so hard to heal.

A light came into his eyes at her arrival. Sliding off Dragon, she put down the supplies and, using sticks and a cord, strengthened the canvas; she pulled more vines across. "Looks like rain," she said. But she kept her distance from where he sat slumped against the low clay cliff. For he did seem stronger.

"What's scaring you?" He blurted the question before she could speak. "You *are* scared, now I can move around." With a little smile, he added, "Well, sort of move."

It was absurd; she wanted to cry. No, to flee—but Sonja hadn't fled. Besides, she had to let him know about those photos. If he was innocent and police searched and found him, he wouldn't even know why.

So she held up the paper from the newstand in Chevy Chase. His eyes scanned the page—the article on "tiger cages" in Saigon, the one about old Bolivian miners, a headline "Witness Confirms Flag Day Bomber I.D." None of it seemed to sink in. "They're hunting you," she said. "Gavin Hareen, it says. It says you bombed an army truck, tearing apart two soldiers and some woman just walking through the park."

He didn't seem to hear, or even to see the photos. "You think that? Of me?"

"Three people." Her voice went hard, but she heard the squishy fear, the awareness of staying safely outside his reach. "That's what they say."

He took the paper, started to read, then looked all around, lips moving like someone stunned. "No—no. They couldn't have thought more than that I was insane." He bit his lips, then went so still she wanted to cover her eyes. "I didn't mean to tell you that." His fingers pulled at tiny stones in the cliffside.

Her heart thumped. Whatever he'd done, she didn't want to find out.

He must have understood. "Just 'cause," he said. "Okay?"

But she had to know. "You better say."

He rolled one of the small stones, white like a miniature marble, between his fingers. "I've done time, is all—stuff against the war. 'Cause I saw, when somebody dies, what happens." He caught his breath. "Don't ever see that. Look, I led a break-in at Port Ruh—we cut the water and stuff. But I got caught. And afterward, when I got out of prison, other things happened, and later I stayed in the park. Under the bridges. It got bad there; I was thinking too much. But it's where I could try to forget."

"Forget?"

He picked up another stone and held it out—smaller, white-pink granite. "Here, you want one?"

She shook her head.

"To forget the stuff that made me do my wrist." Then, before she could ask "But what about the *truck?*" he stretched out his left arm, skinny palm up. A wrinkled scar, something she'd barely noticed among the newer wounds, snaked up his lower arm.

Insane, then, insane. She sat down on a log, suddenly too close but she almost didn't care. "Why?"

"No reason—oh, you know, the usual junk, how my mother died, and how she and Ahmed—my father—how they'd been like dead people." He kept glancing toward the cliff, jiggling the white-pink stone. "All that stuff shrinks say, there in the hospital. Call it the Metal Hospital. There are metal rooms, with lights on all the time." He pressed the smooth edges of the stone with his fingertips. "They said I was paranoid, 'cause I fought; one said depression. I don't think so. I think they can't handle my knowing there's no point."

The mockingbird was at it again. Two shapes like bluejays swung into the dogwoods. "But the truck."

"Truck." He made a sound like a laugh. "I didn't take one step to help them."

"Help who? The guys who—?" But she could not finish. "Why?"

"Why what? My wrist?" He was avoiding her question, like someone guilty. "People always die, see. Ahmed's first family, back in Syria, they got killed. And Mama sick, and later on . . ." His voice wobbled, like someone drowning.

Trying to reach her. Now she couldn't ask about the truck.

"I should have died, you know." He tossed the stone down. "I've done things."

She looked away.

"You think I killed someone."

The bluejays flew off, cawing. He wasn't going to answer about the bombing. And what had he meant, "How my mother died"? The paper said the suspect had been questioned in the past about a death; she had forgotten that.

It was nearly sunset; already, at the stable they'd be wondering, "Malca's got that stallion out late again?" Someone could come looking; the risk to him was enormous. He was aware of it finally, understanding the danger.

"They suspect me." He spoke in a used-up voice. "It would be funny, I guess, if it weren't happening." His eyes unfocused. "Don't you believe all that, okay?"

Awhile later, she said, "Gavin?"

"That's"—he half-laughed, a choking sound—"my name."

She had begun to gather up Dragon's reins, painting the horse with streaks of damp leaves to make it look as if there'd been another fall. "If you didn't do it, you'd better just tell them. Get a lawyer. You can say 'I didn't, it isn't me. I'm not in the People's whatever-it's-called, go ask them.'" But she felt silly saying this, remembering Dad's stories about investigations, back in the old days, and Gerilee's tales of police beating up children in Alabama—not to mention the stuff Mom never spoke of. Still, it didn't make sense. "If a person isn't a criminal . . ."

"I don't think so," he said. He looked strange, sitting there with a hand stretched out. "They won't believe that horse fell." His voice shook with exhaustion—and with the hollowness she didn't want to hear.

THERE WAS A SHADOW MOVING IN THE UPSTAIRS HALL. BEHIND HER, a floorboard squeaked. Dropping the blanket, a warm one she'd found for Gavin to replace the one already ruined by the mud, she spun around. Her mother was standing there, unlit cigarette between her lips. "So what is going on here? You just got fresh laundry." The eyes kept blinking, and Mom's jaw trembled. "This time, no lies. You are my daughter. Also you are distretting your Dad."

Malca tried to think of some way to tell her—to confide, like Anne Frank, or like a daughter in a modern self-improvement book, about this person in the park, and maybe discover unexpected companionship and understanding. But it wouldn't happen. Her mother would think her in danger and call the police.

"Mom." The fear and guilt in her voice did not need pretence. "Mom, yes, there is something . . ." She tried to make the pause sound real.

"I'm waiting, darling."

"I know you don't believe in demonstrations. But there are people—" She scuffed a sandal on the dark gray rug.

"Really?" Mom's laugh was short. "People dying in Vietnam, you mean? And people sitting in, people on a picketline? You know, of course, your Mom does not care to be out there? But maybe I do care, darling, maybe I am very upset this government your Dad sweats his life for keeps on killing people. You are vigiling, right? Where—the White House, like Nina last year?"

Totally weird—Mom was sounding radical. Making it even worse to lie. *But I'm saving someone's life.* "Maybe the White House. I don't know. They just said it could get cold."

"Cold? Not likely." Her mother pulled out a match and lit the cigarette. "No, there is something other—there is something else here. And you understand we cannot go protest—not people in government, not in civil service. You get arrested there and your father and I end up no jobs. No more research, no more curating."

At least Mom was getting back into form, having another panic. "This isn't when you and Dad were young, you know."

The cigarette puffed. "Don't start." Thrusting back her wrinkled neck, squinting, her mother took a long draw. "And don't whine. Please God. I hate it when you wheedle."

You'd hate it lots more if you knew. "I'm not wheedling. But I am going vigiling. All night." Only, all night where? Not in the park, not anywhere near that man. "There's things more important than your and Dad's careers."

"What do you know?" Mom sounded sad. "You sneer at what pays your bills. The foods you fussy children eat, your nice horseback rides. You think college is free?"

"I'm getting a scholarship, remember?" She didn't want to be in this fight.

There was no reply. After a moment, she heard Mom start downstairs. Going out for groceries, probably, or to pick up Dad's dry cleaning—all the usual nonsense they filled their life with to not remember it must end. Malca waited, feeling trapped, until the footsteps passed the kitchen and she heard the back door close.

O.K., Malki. The note, on a square of lined white paper, was scotch-taped to the front of the fridge. Mom was telling her what hadn't been possible to actually say, believing she'd gone into that other, bigger struggle. *Do your Thing, child. Save lives.*

SHE HAD BROUGHT TWO SANDWICHES MADE FROM LAST NIGHT'S ROAST, and it made her happy to sit there and watch him eat so quickly. Only, the trees grew thick around the path and two days ago he'd said, "my mother's death—how she died," as if hinting, and at times his lips moved like someone counting. Or someone crazy, a killer-bomber.

He seemed preoccupied, wiping his mouth on his sleeve and then just resting. "Thank you," he brought out.

It was impossible. "The truck," she said.

He set down the apple juice, but picked it up again. "Guess someone thought he was making revolution."

"'He'? The police say it was you."

"Of course—let everyone think it's antiwar people do the killing. And there I was, former radical leader against Port Ruh, but now a certified lone nut, conveniently out there in the bushes. Listen, you know how streetlights have blue haloes? 'Cause under that light, two army guys were working on that truck and a couple of cops drove past. That's all. And *whoom*, before I could think, everything exploded."

She lifted the sandwich, but the marbled meat looked alive. According to the news, a gun had been found in his tent.

He said, "It could have got me too, you know."

"But those guys, the army guys—"

"Probably trying to fix their engine." He was sucking the last juice into his mouth. "Not to explode themselves, I imagine. Obviously."

Beyond the heat-stifled leaves, the sky reflected in the muddy creek. The article from that morning's *Post* lay crumpled by his blanket. She held it up. "And this, last year? About your mom? It says you told the cops you just found her body lying there. Like you just happened to see that truck—"

"Jesus Christ." He flung down the juice can. "I'm surprised you came back."

For awhile, he lay back on the clay and didn't speak. He pressed his fingertips against his eyelids. "You should be scared, out here. But you don't have to fear me, child."

Child—it made no sense he call her that. Nothing about him made sense, not even his name. *Gavin*—it didn't fit his dark foreignness. But none of this was the real danger.

"Sometimes I did get weird," he said, watching her. "That's true. And I used grass and stuff—not for the music, either. See, there was one point when my mother—she was a ballet dancer—started getting weak, and then weaker until she could hardly move. Her whole world was living death. And then Ahmed walked out. And there we were, trapped in two rooms. I would leave when I could, but someone had to help her. Had to." His eyebrows squeezed into a heavy V, a thick look like a frozen smile. "God, I didn't want to be there. It went on and on. I helped her." He watched a fly buzz in and out among the dogwoods. "Sure. Don't go getting suspicious. Okay?"

The fly arced past the big forsythia. "Later—didn't I tell you this?—I cut my wrist. 'Cause, if I hadn't existed, everyone would have been all right. Obviously, I knew this was a crock—psychoanalytic crud." The creek's tiny gurgle sounded surprisingly loud. "They kept the lights on in those metal boxes. When a door got left open, I ran out. That's all. That's why I hid in the park. Why I lived there." His head moved side to side against the clay. "Why they shot me. I thought."

She heard the catch in his breath, the tiny rasp.

But he hadn't answered about the truck.

"No more," he said. His eyes kept trying to roll back.

"No more—?" she asked.

"Oh—killing."

One of her hands reached out, then, though she knew better, and it landed, awkwardly, on his shoulder. She made herself stay still. And all at once, before she could pull away, he sat up, bending over her other hand, the one with the band-aid on the index finger, and lifted it, as if about to kiss it or something. Blinking, he let go.

Gavin

*W*hether *by sword to end sword, / whether by lies, by paradox, by ends—*

Always, obviously, it turned on issues dead like soldiers. Forced, like all the questions in these stupid songs. Songs died too, all that—the music, political blather, gone down with the running feet, the chants, the frantic race across the Mall in confrontation. Always and forever. Except that he had seen those shreds like meat and there had been no scream.

Whatever logic would devise, the counting could not end. Not after what he'd done.

It did not matter. No time, except to watch for what arrives.

Or if that scrawny, / curves unformed, she /

Shut up, shut up, the girl was helping. Any least consideration—

They would come, guns drawn. Of course.

Malca

Across the lawn, past the maple, gnats swarmed beneath the streetlights. Malca watched through the front screendoor. Better she never return to the park—Eric at the stable always eyeing her, in the gully just dirt and bugs, and Gavin probably lying, and what he'd said today. But it was as if *there* were more real than *here*. She had to understand why he felt so guilty, why he'd grabbed her hand. Someone insane might not even remember if he'd bombed a truck.

No, he couldn't have.

Just as she left the gully, he'd made her take one of the white stones. "You keep this." He'd been coughing. "Not only my guitar—the music was gone. Lives gone." She'd wanted to ask did he mean the war or his mom or what, but she was frightened.

And then what he said was "Don't come here anymore."

She slapped her palm against the screen, not knowing why.

"Is someone out there?" Mom came hurrying down the front hall from the kitchen, wiping the cover of a pot with a damp dishtowel.

"No. Just looking outside." No, he must have said something else. And if she didn't go, he'd probably die.

"Looking at nothing?" Mom kept rubbing the pot cover. The cloth was streaking the shiny steel. "You know, your dad makes jokes, but he worries. We would like you tell us when things go wrong."

"Nothing's wrong." Carefully she paused. "Only . . . why don't you think I'm responsible?"

Mom narrowed her eyes.

"I've a job, I've stuck with it. Gerilee says I'm the best horse trainer they've ever had."

Her mother fished a cigarette out of a pocket. "Someone's saying you're not responsible?"

"No. But I know you and Dad don't trust me, not about serious things. Like driving lessons, or—" She'd borrow the car. Anyplace out of town would be safer for him.

Mom was gazing straight at her. Just holding the cigarette and speaking in the firm voice, like at the office. "High school is not mature enough to drive. You know that. It doesn't matter, Jill in history, Joe in biology, whoever. The answer in our house is no."

"But—" She stopped, hating the whine. In the park, she didn't talk this way.

"Your father's told you. After graduation." Mom lit the cigarette and took a long puff. All at once, her face looked wrinkled like the dishcloth. "So, Malki, how come your indendence means you suddenly need to drive?"

Beyond the screendoor, gnats swarmed. Far off, a siren sounded. The gully was hidden and no one ever took the path there, but for how long?

NINA LIT A JOINT, FACE GLOWING PINK AND YELLOW FROM THE lava lamp. She switched on the rec room stereo. "You want Joni or the Bee Gees?"

"There's someone in the park." Malca pressed her fingertips against the couch arm. "He's sad." *Don't say this.* But if somebody would help— "I gave him a blanket."

Hair wet from a shampoo, Nina knelt behind the tiny bar. She checked the refrigerator for cheese. "Listen, I've discovered a wonderful guy. He organizes farm workers. And when the scabs attacked the line, you should've seen him rush up with a picket sign and—" Balancing two cheeses on her palms, she turned. "Gouda okay?"

The old couch was soft, the square, plaid cushions comfortable.

"Malca, my mother says that sometimes, when we give too much to others, it's a warning we should give more to ourselves."

After the BeeGees, they could play Joan Baez, the one with "Birmingham Sunday" and "Unquiet Grave." And share another joint. "I better leave."

Nina's mouth opened, like a friendly clam. "You're not coming with us to Yellow Submarine?"

Malca slipped her arms into the sleeves of her violet rain jacket. She shook her head.

"Malca, that guy you mentioned, he's not weird or something?"

CHIEF SEEKS MAXIMUM IN TERROR BOMBER CASE. THE HEADLINE ON the *Star* obliterated everything else. She hadn't meant to tell him, or about the ten-thousand-dollar reward or how she always checked behind her, coming here. But she did.

Leaning against the boulder, he put on the shirt she brought, the blue one with a Beatles-style collar that her father had lent her last year. "This is nice," Gavin said. "Now I can let things dry first." He had rinsed out his striped shirt, dragging himself to the creek.

"You've been wearing things wet? You can get sick, that way." Her hand went to her mouth. "Sorry, I sound like Mom."

"Moms." Holding to the boulder, he took a stumbling step. He slid down to the blanket.

"Gavin, there's no one who'll help?"

He pulled a grass stalk and fingered it. "I'm supposed to be a crazy, remember? Suicidal. Why not a bomber too? People should know better, but they don't." He looked hard at her. "Do you? Know anyone, I mean."

Gerilee had "sheltered folks" down South, and there was the guy that Nina used to date, the one who'd driven draftees up to Canada. But they wouldn't deal with a "nutcase," a "killer." *We were pariahs,* Granma had said, one Sunday night, showing her the inlaid heartwood boxes found in Sonja's attic. *Had we not known Sonja so many years, had Sonja not helped us . . . They took her, too.* Mom would watch, the lines by her mouth always deeper. *Malki, you've a big heart, but you do not know this man.*

"Sometimes"—Malca stared at the fugitive, barely three feet away across the muddy ground—"I can't stand my mom." *I lie to her, I laugh at her.* "Her hair's all white. She goes to work, and she comes home. There's nothing left."

He kept twisting the grass stem. It couldn't be that no one else cared.

"Me too," she said, "I mean."

"You what?" He peered into her face.

"*Did* something. I mean, my mom might as well be dead, and I . . ." She'd never told anyone; she didn't know how to start. "Like last New Year's, she got us an ice-cream log, the way they do in France. And I said, 'Wow, look, Hannie, look what the old French poodle brought,' so Mom would have to hear." No, there was no way to explain. "She's wrinkled—she smells like old age. And it isn't Europe did it, it's not her dead people, it's *me*."

Only, here in the thick heat this seemed like a child's problem—far from what he was going through. The police kept searching downtown, going house to house in the Calvert neighborhood, and the woods extended miles each way but they would get here sometime. "Hareen," an FBI guy had told the evening news, "each life you took, we're not forgettin' it."

Only, Gavin didn't seem to be thinking of that now. And he didn't act as if she'd said something childish. She saw tears and thought, though it felt silly, *They're for me.* He pulled himself to one knee, the hurt leg stretched out awkwardly, and bent forward. "I know," he said. "I know." He looked like he might give her a hug or something but she couldn't move away.

"You couldn't kill anyone." She'd wanted him to know that. But her voice was not obeying; it broke into bits. "Gavin, I'm so sorry." She wished he had not done whatever it was.

"Things happen with moms. It's not your doing. Things much worse, they happen. Much worse." But he didn't finish. "See how it pulls on me," he said, and then leaned back, smiling at her. Hiding the fear away. Or something else—some secret.

Any moment, in the sticky heat, police might crash through those trees, come rushing down the gully path.

Very lightly, he patted her hand.

SHE HAD GONE TO THE VIGIL THE FIRST TIME TO COVER HER LIE ABOUT the blanket, but now she *must* go—to find out how people had the courage to do so much against the war. As evening deepened, somebody passed out candles and others read the names of soldiers who'd been killed, pointing the megaphone toward the windows of the White House. An old, short-haired woman standing near her spoke of someone named Emma Goldman, and Malca asked, "Who's that?"

"A great anarchist who gave up everything. But surely you knew that."

She looked down, embarrassed. "I'm not a very political kind of person."

"'Kind of person'? That's exactly the way they divide us."

"C'mon, lay off, she's a kid." The speaker was a young guy, rugged in an army jacket with a flag painted upside-down. "Besides, how they really get us is fear." He gave Malca a quick grin.

"You're sure, Paul?" The old woman shook out her long grey hair. "And what of guilt? Since everybody feels guilty—over one thing if not another."

Like Gavin does? Malca took two steps away. But Paul was ripping open a paper bag and rolling a joint. He took a drag, passed it on. Crickets trilled in the bushes. Catching her glance, Paul grinned again. She looked down; then she picked up a picket sign and started to walk back and forth, stopping occasionally to rub sweat from her hands. They were clean hands, not grubby with clay and blood like Gavin's. Another man had joined Paul and now they opened a bottle of wine, smiling at each other. Someone was singing "Joe Hill."

As night wore on, people huddled in groups. They told stories, lots of stories—many about antiwar marches, and some about unions; others recounted struggles in the South. Once, a blonde woman spoke of "the night the jeeps got wasted and the power vanished, over at Port Ruh," and Malca felt strangely proud.

"Hey, man, those were dropout crazies." It was the guy standing with Paul who spoke; then someone else chimed in. Malca wanted to argue, but they might catch on. After awhile, she asked the blonde woman, who sat crosslegged by a circle of thin candles, "What's Port Ruh?"

"That big Navy base on Chesapeake Bay." The woman yawned. "These kids—well, *you* wouldn't call them kids—couple years ago got over the fence and knocked out the electric current and . . . Well, I forget exactly. It was brilliant, though—the sort of action that shows the machine is vulnerable, but that doesn't itself do violence. Not to people. You don't remember?"

"I was mostly into horses then." The candles flickered.

All around, people sang. There were more stories—tales of rent strikes in Chicago, resistance in the Rockies, blocking busloads of draftees. Later someone spoke of anarchy, a world without rules or war, based instead on mutual care. It didn't speak to how to know life's meaning, or what could give a person courage like Sonja's, or even how to stop any way. But the next day, when she mentioned it to Gerilee, the stable manager replied, "Like, there's all kinds of folks in the Movement, but I don't remember any anarchists sittin' in with us, or marchin' at my side the day we walked in Selma." Then Gerilee reached up by the *Feeding and Stabling* manuals on the office shelf and pulled, from a bunch of pamphlets and papers, a thin book called *The Anarch: Eight Essays*.

"This explains—?" Malca began, but the red phone rang, and Gerilee wiggled her thumb impatiently, *Go wait out in the corridor.*

Probably an irate parent. Malca could hear Gerilee's deep voice rise, murmuring in a sweet and feminine tone, "Oh yes of course—well certainly, for sure."

The corridor sloped down toward the boarders' box stalls, and Malca stepped over to pet Enticement, the thoroughbred whose owner lived in France. She was stroking the animal's forehead when she heard the East Paddock door open. Gerilee must have finished really fast. But, no, it was Eric, bumping through the archway, carrying two of the new London saddles.

"Here, I'll help." She started forward. After all, Eric could be sweet when he was sober, helping with the littles, showing her and Dante, the assistant groom, his architecture drawings. But Eric had stopped still and stared. "Look at you," he said. He spoke thickly and, when he whistled, it sounded gross. Like a comic book. Thinking he was trying to be funny, she smiled. But he wasn't. Head down, tilted a little sideways, he started toward her.

She backed away, bumped against Enticement's stall. A splinter caught at her palm.

"Hey, Eric—" Gerilee was hurrying down the corridor. "Damn, Eric, where you putting that goddamn tack? We got another carload to bring in today."

Malca couldn't see the groom's face—Gerilee had stepped in front of her—but she heard him say something like "Sneaks around here, Ger, like a you-know-what."

"Malca, go get me Misty's chart. Dragon's too, please. Oh, and Sky Beyond's." Gerilee spoke without turning, her voice stiff. "You'll find them on my desk tray, thanks. Now, Eric, how about we stop the fiddling and get in that tack before it rots?"

GAVIN WAS SO HAPPY WITH THE RAZOR AND MIRROR SHE'D BROUGHT him that she couldn't look away.

"If I did get a lawyer?" he was saying. "'Cause they'd never let it come to trial. They keep saying a bomb, but maybe that engine could have . . . Listen, you ever heard of any 'People's Liberation Tribe'?" He stood the mirror and razor on a rock and smiled at them.

Search Expands—the papers kept printing numbers for phoning in tips. The wound in his thigh was closing, but the leg was still too numb; he couldn't stand. "Like trying to heave a log around," he'd called it.

She drew a breath. "Gavin, I've been thinking. That was an army truck, after all, and if bombing it could help stop the war—"

"Stop the war?" He turned the mirror over. He wasn't smiling anymore. Beyond him, water glinted, light overlaid with leaves; clouds heaped into the sky. "I made a decision, once."

"In Warsaw, my uncle shot a Nazi."

"It's done," he said, and then, as if still not believing it, "Malca, they didn't say 'Stop,' they yelled, 'Hey you, hey you,' and started shooting." He picked at his wrist, but there was nothing on it. "See, even if I did get acquitted, you know where I get put?" The empty shadow crossed his eyes. "Back in that hole. Dear child, I'd rather die."

"I'm not a child." Then she blushed. Dumb thing to say.

Only, it had made him smile again, and this time she was so glad that she smiled, too.

When, soon after, a crack of thunder sounded, seeming very close, and she looked up, away from Gavin, she realized they had been sitting smiling at each other the whole time. Before she could look away again, afraid he might say something, the first drops of rain began to fall. She felt them on her face, and one ran down his cheek while another—they both laughed—rolled along his nose.

"They'll expect you, won't they, Malca? Better get that horse in dry."

Starting toward Dragon, she turned, too quickly, to look behind. But if Gavin noticed, he showed nothing. He had got under the shelter, and hunched up against the blowing rain. She wished he wasn't hunted and his story made more sense—that he made more sense and it didn't seem he said things sometimes just to make her believe him, and there wasn't always the *something* that he hadn't said.

That night she dreamed she was driving Gerilee's Dodge, frantic because a person lay all bloody on the backseat and she hadn't used more care, and from behind there loomed a creature red and black, but it was Gavin, and he said she had lost everything.

She woke up frightened, but by afternoon the gully felt tranquil as they spoke beside the creek. She'd brought hamburgers and fries, still warm, and while they ate they watched the stallion graze, coming closer and closer.

"May I pet him?" Gavin's question surprised her. Mouth full, she nodded. It was true, he never had. He reached out a hand and Dragon snuffed, whickering as the fingers rubbed the sensitive spot between his eyes. She couldn't look away, but finally the horse gave a snort and moved off, still grazing, toward the stream.

"Malca, thank you," Gavin said.

She looked down. Truly, the affection, or whatever it was, was so obvious. Crunching up the empty hamburger wrapper, she carefully wiped her mouth, pressing the old kleenex against her lips. Gavin had lifted his right hand and she thought crazily that he was about to rub between *her* eyes or something. But he was watching Dragon, who had raised his head, ears alert.

A minute or two later, though, the stallion went back to grazing, the gully again grew somnolent and still, and she found herself caught in the serious gaze of this black-eyed man people said might be a terrorist and murderer. He was speaking of what he called "that goddamn war," of how she hoped to be a doctor and why he'd once thought to be a scientist, and, as much as he could remember, about something called "Schröedinger's cat," which was confused, and black holes.

Then Gavin said, "You'd look good in a hat," and put the worn-out neckscarf on her hair, and she pulled it off so fast he burst out laughing. Only for an instant, though—someone might ride past on Western Trail.

But it was hard—they kept thinking up jokes—not to keep laughing. She wanted to stay, but then he said, "Malca, that sun is nearly setting," and she knew she had to leave.

Gavin

In simplest terms, it was ridiculous; those songs had been false hope, the body's struggles to survive. Nevertheless, if one is granted a generous mind, it soon becomes incumbent, no matter what contingencies, to work for necessary good. And naturally one argues such a statement has no meaning, yet acuity requires every generous deed, no matter how abhorrent, that arises from such clear necessity.

Or some conclusion of that sort. Obviously. What must be done.

There he had halted, every night—the thick park nights of humid spring before the blue flash—aware lucidity too often fled into the darkness. For, after all, the basic theory in its origins had been *comparison*, or rather *in comparison*, a simple recognition that, amid the count—the sea—of millions dying in this war, one death or even two were droplets, nothing in comparison. So that it was all right if he—it would be fine, indeed incumbent, that to end the massacre he—

Here too, each time, he'd halted, aware that such conclusion must— here, counter-theory entered, blaring trumpets—*had to* imply that simple counting could encompass any person's universe, that it was possible to redo what a death must end. Which clearly must be false.

Sometimes when night faded he forgot all this, instead counted leaves. The pallid dogwood blossomed in a different universe, a world hard-edged—that girl, his lost guitar, those memories of rampant theorizing in the damp tent with the wires waiting and the bullets.

Red with mud, his hands clenched.

Through the long chain of events, he had at first been paralyzed— now it was obvious—by all that past, by Mama's tears and Ahmed's haunted mumblings in the blue chair, later caught up in the militance, the street fights, and the crazed commune, each night a new experiment in screwing—Selena the Bead Queen, Left-Coast Jack, the rest—and writing lyrics and pretending joy. Until he learned that, though the counting of the dead might have no exit, yet he must work for a wider whole, since only theory urged *comparison,* or *in comparison.*

Wearily, he raised his head, leaned forward to push the stones around their tiny circles, numbers crawling higher as his fingers pinched the gritty objects—leaves, twigs, red clay—into dried shapes like flat body-bags, sticks piled like towers. He still fell if he tried to turn over. The wounds waited, poised to open. No one had screamed when the truck went up. Each pill, he'd placed with clear precision.

And what the fuck did you expect?

Malca

Yellow flowers gleamed in the late sunlight, but even as she walked, the air grew dark. Pussywillows bent in the rising wind. She had to keep alert here, and around Gavin, too. He understood so much, but when he'd said that cops might have rigged the truck "to set off the bomb and get their Movement patsy," she'd remembered an article she'd read on "complex paranoid" delusions. Or he might be simply lying. She hesitated. Here the creek turned south, and vines obscured the banks, where anyone could lurk; two days before, beside the paddock fence, she'd seen eyes watching.

Only, she had to know what Gavin was going through—she could never have endured it. Again she started forward, shifting her little pack, rain poncho slung across one shoulder.

Beyond, the route turned slippery, squeezed onto a rocky margin between the water and the bank; she grabbed at branches, trying not to fall. The wind was cold and she pushed against it. There were two more bends before she reached the rocky outcrop at the gully's mouth. She peered up its banks, seeking to pierce the veil of leaves above the tarp.

The glade was empty.

And then she saw him. Deep in the shadows, he crouched by the creek's edge, struggling to get to his feet. "You," he said, eyes watery with relief. Not looking, he began to pull himself up toward the shelter, then lay there full-length on the ground. He pulled the blanket to his neck. "I should not have got so scared," he said.

All around, the grass bent in the heavy wind. She stepped closer and leaned over, starting to tuck the blanket tight to keep him warm.

"No." He lifted a warning hand.

"Not your fault," he added. He sounded awful. Half-turned away, he stared into the vines. Overhead, wind rattled through the oaks. "They are going to find me."

She shook her head.

"Malca, listen. Hear that storm coming? It is dangerous for you here."

She could put her hands around his wrists, say *Dangerous for you too.* Bending sideways, she reached toward her rolled-up poncho. "I have to know what it's like. Being here."

"You can't know."

"It's okay, Mom thinks I'm at the vigil."

Suddenly he pulled himself up to a sitting position, wounded leg extended. "No. No, Malca, I have told you. It is dangerous."

"I have to know—"

"Go home." His hands twisted a copper wire from his pack.

"—to know what you mean."

"Go home." She stumbled backward, half-tripping on a fallen branch. But he didn't look up. His lips moved silently, and his fingers kept twisting the wire.

The whole way back upstream, the thickets hung so dense she barely made out the cliffs. If Gavin could turn cold like this, anything could happen. In fifth grade, her friends Roxie and Jill had said, "Go get yourself some other friend." The police said Gavin had kept a loaded pistol in his tent. He'd had those wires with him the night of the explosion. Guitar-string wires, he called them. He could be anyone. But was it so terrible, really, that bombing?

She had barely arrived at the road to the Beltway when the cloudburst opened up.

"I'M GLAD YOU'D THE SENSE TO COME HOME, BUBBIE, WITH THIS weather." Dad opened the screen door and lifted the wet blanket from her shoulders. She pulled off her dripping poncho. From upstairs came some cello concerto, probably the Dvorak; Mom must be lying down.

"Don't let that cat—" Dad stuck out a foot, blocking the soaked tabby from slinking through the doorway. "Your mother has enough work without cleaning up after your strays."

Purring, the cat twisted as she lifted him, and batted at her with a soft white paw.

"Another thing, Bubbie."

She curled her fingers around the wet paw, feeling the claws retract. The purr became a rumble. Guitar wires—that was all.

"Another thing, isn't that top a little low to go around in, at night? Your mom and I may have to reconsider some of our policies, if you don't start taking better care of yourself."

GAVIN DIDN'T LOOK UP; SHE TRIED NOT TO NOTICE. FINALLY HE SAID he'd heard people walking down Western Trail during the night, soon after the rain, stopping sometimes as if to search for something, or for some other reason.

"Tell me what's in your book, Malca."

It was *The Anarchs.* She began to read aloud. The author spoke of social structures and human innocence. What if those searchers had followed her here?

"Malca, I am sorry about last evening."

The leaves were full of moisture; she wondered how it could be possible. Some had long streaks of aqua green.

"See, it was dangerous. And you weren't getting it."

"You scared me."

"Did I?" Too quickly, he turned away, whittling a piece of wood; she watched him shape it. His knife no longer bothered her; she could not even remember when she'd first noticed it. It had been there in the grungy leather pack—strange he'd had that with him—along with the wires and a twenty-dollar bill. "You take this," he'd said one time, pulling out the bill, trying to hand it to her. "I am tired of you spending money on me."

"But"—she hadn't wanted to worry him, only it was the truth—"you'll need it if they come." She'd pushed the money back. "In case you have to flee."

Mom and Granma had fled to Sonja's with only their hats and coats. In Gavin's pack, there'd been two pairs of socks, soaked and ruined. The book had survived, though; he kept it under the tarp. It looked like a diary but long and narrow, with a brown patch where his blood had leaked through. And the map was whole, showing someplace in the northern Colorado Rockies.

Now, smiling a little, he put down his knife and the bit of wood, watched her a moment, then spread the map out on the ground. "Come look," he said. Pointing to a town partway up the map, he ran his finger along a trail and started to explain the topo lines.

"I know about those," she said. "We practiced maps in riding camp."

"Well, see that lake? There, beside the trail—White Summit Lake. I went there once. It's over ten thousand feet, and the mountains reach thirteen. And that's a huge main trail, but—it is incredible—half a mile away you are deep into the wilds."

She hugged her arms. "You're going there, aren't you? Instead of—you know—trying to reach Mexico? Or looking for your Dad?"

He didn't reply. He rolled the map and lifted up the wood, curving his blade in short, quick flashes down the grain. The sun was low, shadows crossing the creek. She tried again. "Your dad, where was he from?"

"Everywhere, the whole eastern Mediterranean." Gavin was studying the wood, working it. "Until he turned himself to nothing. 'Cause he would sit in that apartment every evening and he'd stare somewhere—stare into his dead." He lowered his knife to the clay. "I won't turn to nothing, like that."

But you keep staring into such a place. "And your mom?" she said.

"Mama? She was American, pure Irish and Italian Catholic and one-fourth Black Southern Baptist. People used to say we . . . Never mind. Racism was part of it." Suddenly he smiled and held up the carving; his eyes shone. "Look, Malca, a blackbird! Sort of."

She stretched out a hand. "See those claws!" Her fingers trembled, touching the wood. Whatever else, being here was all she wanted. With someone who knew what it was to feel alone and guilty, who understood. She placed the carving on the grass and sat stroking it in silence.

He turned to her, so warmly that she looked away. "Oh, Malca."

But she opened two cans of Pepsi and just said, "I always beat the boys in chess club." After awhile, he told her about having gone to college on a scholarship but left, "'cause tuition still got too expensive, and Ricardo—a friend, you know?—got drafted and got killed, and every night you'd see the war on television. I clerked for a year; that was dumb." He said he'd played guitar at night and written songs. "We were a band—not acoustic, either. Later, they went to San Francisco."

Stories from before—that was what he called it, *before*. Other stories, too—about Port Ruh, and sleeping in crashpads, fighting cops at demonstrations. But when she touched his hand and asked about the songs, first he clasped her fingers and then he pulled away and said, "They're lost." And when she asked, "You still like guitar?" he answered, "C'mon, don't," and looked drained.

MOM HANDED HER ANOTHER DISH TO DRY. "I DON'T LIKE YOU GOING out so often we don't know where. And that vigil—it's too much risk. Soon they'll make camps."

"Camps?" Malka ducked her head, hiding the smile and looking down into the soapy water. It was all Mom's way to protect her, holding the worry-gate ready to slam down; she'd felt far less guilty since figuring this out. Yet it also meant that anything she did could wipe Mom out. Only, she hadn't known Mom had heard all those warnings, the stuff people talked about while holding signs and looking toward the White House—rumors of crackdowns, arrests, "internment camps." But "camps" were where Granpa Chaim had vanished, Chaim-the-great, Mom and Aaron-the-brave's dad. It was Grandpa Chaim who had stood in line every day trying to get visas, chasing after passports for his family. "But he was too honest," Granma had said, "so we did not get out." While Granma lay dying, she kept calling, "Chaim, Chaim, where are you?" Camps were where Granma and Mom had been taken, finally, and probably Sonja-the-archivist, Granma's friend, who hid them.

Mom was passing her the knives and spoons and forks. She didn't know why she had to know, but she must. Dad was out; he couldn't stop her. "Mom?" She tried to make her voice thoughtful, respectful. "How did Granma and you get caught? What happened to Sonja?"

Mom was humming, pulling a cup and saucer from the suds. With her other hand, she reached, not looking, for a cigarette. She scraped a match against the matchboook. "Dead is dead." She blew the smoke in a thin ring across the sink toward the dark mirror of the window. "Sometimes it worked for them, to be unreasonable." The hand moved back and forth, signaling, and Malca passed a freshly washed ashtray.

"But what happened?"

Eyes taut across, her mother shook the ashes to the sink. "First we had a hoping time."

You want to kill your mother? Stop this!

"Mom, Sonja must have known you and Granma might still be all right. Doesn't that count?" She wanted to say something reassuring.

"We each have our contingency, darling. *You're* here, that's the important thing." Then Mom's eyes shifted slightly, like a waking cat's. "So, Malki, what makes you ask?"

Mom, he's my friend. He used to write songs. Nobody ever walked on Western Trail. Somebody help us.

Gavin

Goddamn the ants, but at least he had got her to bring bugspray. He did not know how he could have managed weeks of this. Three weeks, four—whatever it had been. This filthy muck, mosquitoes, the ugly rasp from his own throat. He squeezed his fists against the grass, pressed his face into the familiar shawl. At least he could keep things clean now—limp around instead of flop. Like a fish, he had been, or a flapping, chewed-on bird. His leg still twisted, struggling to climb Mount Everest when he tried to walk. Yet to escape—

Here in this swamp, when he looked for trees against the night stars there was only pink haze and recently the sallow moon on its way to full. In the day, at any sound he dragged the stinking canvas, weighted with its crackling camouflage of dusty leaves, to crouch against this mud cliff, every grubby thing he owned squeezed under his knees. Two or three times, some days—even before those searchers, or whoever, had gone down that trail. For in this paradoxic universe there was no strong defense for a creature that could not run.

Sometimes he was so weary with it he dozed, indeed like a sick creature, heart racing into the imaginary road, *away away, hurry hurry, get out get out.* If they found him—*taking it all into account*—they could not let him live.

He tried to force the angle of a branch, the outline of a leaf, from the muggy night. Too helpless here, dependent. *This is how Mama must have felt.* And Ahmed had left, but two years later had returned, staying only long enough to be loved again—long enough to promise Mama, and to father that baby who did not live, the one whose body had been placed in the small black metal box. Long enough to say, while Mama lay shuddering and emptied, "I think yes, better we had had none."

Long enough to start the horrors. *Ahmed, Papa, I remember wondering what you knew, and your face in the crowd beside the ambulance.*

Screw—none of that crap mattered now. He had seen a foot fly, legless, and a roasted arm, in the blue-lit night. More than anything, he wanted to get up and, like a normal person, walk away from here. He stuffed the end of the shawl into his mouth. Walk away from this thick red clay. From himself.

And from that creature, fragile, asking things she must not. He would have liked to simply know her, not need her help for every smallest thing. When she was present, he forgot it awhile, the "You're who should have died, Gav," the red pills, the waiting and the blue explosion, chain of numbers, and all that ensued, and then the curling-up, the giving-in—and horror afterward when he would realize what all this was doing to his chance to live.

In this terror, sometimes he heard footsteps, but one evening it had been her slim pale form, wanting to stay with him through a soaking thunderstorm. He did not remember what they'd said, thinking only of those glimpses of her breasts below the ruffle of the low-cut blouse even while her narrow hand had reached out to his blanket. But she was young, so innocent and scared—yet wanting to know what the world was like, not to leave him alone to it. She had watched him from quiet brown eyes. "No," he had said, too sharply.

And the next day, she had started in again, "Why?" and "How can we know life's meaning?"

He had spoken without thinking, stupidly—"I think you know, if anyone does"—and then gone cold. Because she had blushed and it made her face look elegant and pretty. So he had not answered seriously, not asked even "Meaning to whom?" or any of the rest, or told her of the count, but instead had snapped "Aren't you lucky to be safe enough to worry over such questions?" Wanting to say "Your heart is beautiful." Wanting to touch the narrow silky ribbon of the neckline. Barely formed—unaware of her own responses.

Here, the dark was too thick. In the mud, he had pushed to one side all the bits of sticks, the pinched-up leaves and clay. There was no time left to imagine, no longer continents of hope. Once he had been like Malca, exploring those questions, seeking the whole universe. Once—before he had decided and had thrown away this life they now must work so hard to save.

Malca

"Lousy disguise, huh?" Gavin's beard was still mostly stubble. Earlier, he'd asked her to get him "a pair of shades, something plastic and straight-looking," and roadmaps. Only, there was no safe place for him to go. No strength, either; yesterday, for the first time, he'd managed to limp part way up the gully. And his mind—often it too seemed trapped here. Now he dropped a leaf into the current, and they watched it whirl atop an eddy; he tossed in a smaller leaf so it hit the main surge, riding a crest until it disappeared. He cleared his throat. "You do realize you'll want other things, after college. To teach people. You won't want—"

She had been reading an epistemology book. "That's the future. It can't make sense to 'know our future.'" A thread was loose on the ruffle of her new blouse; she twisted it between her fingertips.

"Malca, they might not find me."

The clouds always made the woods dark. She couldn't look at him or speak. Waterbugs hovered over the eddy. He said there had been the night sounds again, this time on the far bank, and not so near, but he could make out a flashlight going back and forth in a meadow just past the woods.

"Fellows working hard out there"—he was trying to turn it into a joke—"still chasing their bomber." He took a step in her direction, then another, face pale.

"No one ever came here." She shook her head. Stupid tears again. "Not since I was thirteen. No one."

"Well, been lots busier lately." He grinned, but his eyes said something very different.

"Only you."

"Malca—" He'd reached the oak beside her. He stood unmoving, like someone lost. Years before, she had got lost once, in Hecht's department store, full of Christmas decorations. People had found her. "Be careful," she said. When he leaned forward, she felt something touch her hair. Reaching up, she found a leaf there, like the ones he had been dropping in the water.

"The F.B.I.," she said, holding the leaf between her fingers, unsure whether to put it back on her hair. "They're worse than police. They have these secret methods for catching people—lab tests and everything. In eighth grade, we took a tour." Ridiculous. But she had to warn him.

He had come closer; even the hollows of his cheeks were smiling. "Did they? And they told you about the magic potion? And how they slip in when you least expect it, and catch you in your sleep?"

"Cut it out, Gavin." Only, her hair tingled; it felt weird, electric. And suppose there were magic leaves, and if you laid them on someone's forehead, he could become invisible and never be found.

IT WAS STRANGE, SEEING THE STABLE MANAGER SO OUT OF CONTEXT, here at the vigil, carrying a handmade "Bring the Troops Home Now" sign. Malca held her candle in its paper windshield, talking with the Cuban lady with the silver rings, and the conscientious objector Jason, and then Amanda, who was twenty-two and beautiful and nice to everybody. When a police helicopter hovered, people laughed, "Smile for the camera," but Amanda, her pretty face tilted skyward, said, "Those always make me think of peasants being chased through the jungle like prey."

Malca looked around. She hadn't realized, but she would miss these people if she left. They were planning civil disobedience for Nagasaki Day, and Amanda had asked her to join them in climbing over the White House fence in silent witness, "though we'll likely only get arrested. I don't know the point, some days." Hearing what they would risk, knowing what Gavin had risked already, was changing her, she thought; now she understood better how urgent it all was. But if she were arrested, she could no longer help Gavin. Still, he didn't need help so much anymore. His beard was growing, and he studied the roadmaps and tried hard to walk; yesterday he'd told her he felt strong. But now there was more danger, the cops doing sweeps.

"That horse has done you wonders, Malca." Gerilee placed her placard along the fence with the others, and took up one of the candles. Around them, several people were singing "Give Peace a Chance."

"I've been antiwar so long," Gerilee confided, "I must know most folks around." Tilting her head, she added quietly, "And some of them may have ways to help your little resister—or draft dodger, whatever you got." Gerilee's candle flickered in its holder against the rising wind. "Just no Weathermen, okay? No crazies, sort of thing. Don't get me wrong, I'm not opposed to action, but . . ." She leaned closer. "Anyhow, I've been sensing something."

A sweet, high voice, Amanda's or the little woman Emily's, was beginning the first verse of "We Shall Overcome." People linked arms. Gerilee whispered, "Like, Eric tells me he sees you carting stuff. He said, 'What's with that girl?' He's got his own things going, I know, and he never figures the whole of anything, but I sure can. Want me to check around? Discreetly."

She'll protect her stable first. That had been Gavin's warning, the one time she'd suggested that Gerilee might help. "I don't understand," she answered. People were raising their candles aloft before the gates. "No. Please, Gerilee."

Everyone was singing, and soon they began "Down by the Riverside" and "We Shall Not Be Moved." Malca's eyes filled, but Gerilee's deep voice joined two other women's in "Masters of War" and then in a sort of wailing people said came from the movie *Battle of Algiers*.

On the bus home, rain gusting, Malca shivered and sweated, jacket wrapped around her waist, and worried over and over about Gerilee's words and about that fugitive, no safe draft dodger or resister, who *must not* be a murderer and who was Gavin and alone.

AND EVEN IF HE'D DONE THAT BOMBING, IT HAD BEEN TO STOP THE WAR —which vigiling couldn't. But whatever he'd done, whatever lived in him as emptiness, today it made a hollow of his voice. At first he'd said, "All right, there may be someone—all right, at least they'll never snitch," but now, an instant later, "No, forget it, I don't want you implicated more. And yet—" And then, "There must be a way. We can—"

Around and around. That back and forth that came upon him like the hollowness. Or was he just trying protect her? But there was no time left. Twice this week at the stable, she'd caught Eric watching her, just hanging out beside the hay bales checking up on everything she did. And there'd been boot prints in the mud right where the game path entered Western Trail. Risks stood all around, like the dogwoods on the far bank, their brown petals fallen to the earth. "I'm ready, Gavin," she said.

The creek's reflections shimmered across Gavin's face; their patterns floated back and forth. "All right," he said. "Let's start with Maura. Her line may be bugged, but she is solid. More than solid."

All at once, Malca's head felt thick, like getting a very bad cold. "Maura?"

"Works for *Freedom News*." He was scraping something, a bit of clay, off his sleeve. "An old girlfriend—nice person."

"You miss her." It was a dumb remark.

"We were friends."

She saw a dead gnat near his elbow. She should say so, say *Look out, a gnat*. "I've never had a boyfriend."

"I know."

But he wasn't paying attention, just watching her lips. They were ugly, far too wide. "Wipe the gnat off," she said.

But, instead, he turned and limped toward his pack. Bending awkwardly, holding to a tree so his bad leg wouldn't slip, he reached inside and pulled out his old notebook. He tore off a page and wrote something down, then held the paper toward her. "See, a phone number—just like in the movies. Seriously, memorize it and then tear the whole page into molecules." His voice sounded flat, like someone's in an office. "Supposed to be a safety measure. And hang up if someone asks where you are. Immediately."

He reached out a hand, and for a moment she thought he'd changed his mind and wanted the paper back.

Instead, he touched her arm. "Malca. Be safe."

TWO HOURS LATER, IN A HOT PHONEBOOTH FAR ENOUGH DOWN Connecticut Avenue not to give away his location, she dialed the number. The sun was setting, and glaring streaks from a passing bus rolled over the glass. Reflections from the creek had gleamed along his face.

After five rings, a woman answered.

"Maura?" Malca stared into the metal corner of the booth. Again a bus stopped, motor grunting; it was hard to hear.

"Speaking." The voice was warm, womanly.

There was a phrase Gavin had said to use, "I'm calling back about the oranges." Malca's fingers played along the coils of the cord.

"Oranges? Very nice, thank you. Except . . ." A throaty voice. "Of course, these days I've a first-rate banana."

But then, instead of hanging up, the woman coughed, like clearing her throat, and the whole tone changed. "Wait—excuse me. Please, wait. I'm sorry, especially"—the voice went deeper—"since everybody, everyone, down where I work, is speaking of the coming harvest. It'll be big, they say. And harvest time is coming fast."

"When?" But the phone went dead. Malca lowered the receiver. She had understood—but so could anyone bugging the line.

When she reached Three Star Grocery, where Dad used to take her for ice cream in third grade, she bought a coke. "Jason went south to start a business," Gavin had said, and Annie, whoever she was, was in India studying with a famous guru. Gavin's dad was alive, "but certainly his line will be bugged, and besides . . ." There was no one else.

She had been careful, the call quick, but in his old group's code, "oranges" meant Gavin. If any agent was listening, now the harvesters would know that Gavin was alive and somewhere near and help was needed.

GERILEE LOOKED UP FROM CRACKING HER KNUCKLES AND RAN A LENGTH of halter leather between her fingers. "Come here," she said, voice gone gruff; Malca followed, away from where anyone might hear. "You know," Gerilee began, "I've a mind for puzzles. That's how I keep this place—with my eyes and my head." She leaned against the fence, and Malca sat on the square little stand that children used to reach the stirrups, what some staff called the dude-step. "You know I got a pretty good idea what's up."

"Nothing is up."

"Don't lie, hon." The stable manager twisted the piece of leather and stretched both arms over the top rail like a middle-aged cowgirl, looking toward where a class of new riders, ten- and eleven-year-old girls, saddled-up and nervous, led their beginners' nags around the "tot-pen." In the paddock, four horses grazed, the yellow-white mane of the stallion tossing among them.

"I'm not real comfortable about Eric these days." Gerilee spoke as if to herself. "When he gets a thing for somebody . . ." She straightened. "If it comes to it, Malca, if you need to—when the time comes—take the horse."

TAKE THE HORSE. IT WAS SAD—GERILEE HAD BELIEVED IN HER WHEN nobody else did, but now there was so much the stable manager just didn't get. Sighing, Malca leaned on the bough beside the swirling creek. Gold glints shone in the water. She glanced back at Gavin.

The skin around his eyes was grey from nights of keeping watch. "You think I didn't hear you sing to me?" he said. He was scraping the last visible stains from the pack, but blood still stuck, like sap on silver maple bark, to the front of the journal. "It was Mama's book about being sick," he'd told her, "and Ahmed put notes in, too, and later I stuck songs there. It's what was in my pack; it's what is left."

Watching his quick movements, she clenched her hands around the whittled blackbird. She knew why he was giving her a present now.

He limped over to sit across from her on the muddy grass. The sun sparkled on the water in the distance beyond his face. His hand reached slowly in a strumming motion, like playing a guitar chord. "The worst nights, I would remember the songs. I wrote a few, you know."

His lost songs—he's redoing them. He sounded quietly happy in a way she'd never heard.

"You know?" He made another pretend strum, still listening for noises in the woods, and then began to sing, but very quietly. "We'll build a new world"—his fingers moved, intent, on the imaginary guitar—"free of war's horrors / free of cruel sorrow / There will come tomorrow." He glanced up. "That's the start, anyhow."

A few yards away, Dragon snuffed, kicking out at something.

Almost shyly, Gavin smiled at her; he bent his head. He did four more pieces, but the lyrics were dark. "Oh, the soldier," he sang finally, "the soldier, he kept / trying, trying"—the words told of a G.I. struggling to save a woman and child from a burning "hootch," trying over and over, long after it must have been too late—"but the roof, the straw, swayed / swaying, swaying, / and the roof, the roof fell /down, down on / his own land . . ."

"Gavin." Her voice was a whisper. "Gavin, that person's you."

On the phantom guitar, he picked a final chord. His mouth turned down. "Don't be so sure. See, people always find theories. Like, that first song, the one you liked? It's not even my own music; it's from an old tune—listen." He sang it again, but this time the original words, in a jangly, twanging voice, drawing each phrase out longer and longer until finally he was laughing too hard to sit up. And so was she, hand gripping his, flat against the muddy grass. They held tightly, fingers to wrist, wrist to fingers, lying there helpless because they couldn't, either one, let go. "Yes, but soon"—Gavin raised himself up, and laughed a little—"soon it's time to flee the harvest, even to nowhere-land."

HER FIRST THOUGHT WAS *IT COULDN'T HAVE BEEN NINA, NINA WOULD never tell—and anyhow she didn't know anything.* And not Hannah—Hannah could get angry fast, but Hannah wasn't vicious. More likely Eric or—probably Eric; someone had been watching. She had glimpsed somebody, Tuesday morning, in the woods behind the stable, though when she turned in the saddle, no one was there and, for safety, she stayed away from Gavin's hideout the whole day.

Standing now in the front hall, she watched Dad's face past the diningroom doorway while he listened. He was clutching the receiver hard, and she knew—even before she heard him say, voice strained like a turtle's, "He told them *Malca?* Miss Tassavera, he said *Malca's* involved? But that's insanity." Dad was taking off his gold glasses, grasping them with the same hand as the phone, and with the fingers of his other hand he was pressing the skin around his eyes. "Miss Tassevara, why should anyone believe this fellow? You don't, yourself, or you'd hardly have listened-in like that—would you?" Now his mouth turned hard, nose stiffening like a crow's beak. "No. No, Malca wouldn't know a person like that. She's a student—a good girl."

Dad, please don't work so hard for me. But she dared not cry out; if he saw her, he'd try to stop her. Gerilee must be trying to send a warning—*Eric's told the cops*—but it was Gavin who had to be warned. Immediately.

She was out the front door before Dad noticed. No one was around. Someone might be watching, but she saw only the usual cars parked along the curbs. Pretending to search for a lost kitten, she passed the Miltzers' house and the Robinsons' bungalow, then turned into the alley toward Brandywine Street. Calling softly, "Here kitty, here kitty," she went another five or six blocks, keeping to alleys and swinging her Indian cloth purse, humming like someone preoccupied and happy. She took a diagonal path across an empty lot to Connecticut Avenue, trying to think of some route that could avoid the L bus. And then she understood—they didn't have to follow her; they could just wait near the stable and trail her from there.

Or Eric might already have shown them where to look.

THEY HADN'T GOT THERE, THOUGH. NOT YET. "I BROUGHT STUFF on Dragon," she panted. She slid from the stallion's back. Gavin stood, hands white-knuckled around a branch, realizing.

She was sweaty in the old bellbottoms and too-warm shirt. "Dragon just cantered up to me, like he knew. He was in the north paddock—I didn't go near the stable, I wouldn't have. Here, here's food, things I hid. Come, I'll help. We can get away." She handed him the large sack, watched his right hand grasp it. Too late now to take back her words.

"And how, may I ask?" He just stared at her. "You've brought a car? Or you meant to use that horse?"

But even before he stopped speaking, he had lowered the sack and stepped close; she felt his hands stroking her hair. "Oh Malca, no no—I am sorry. Truly." There were crickets in the mud by the edge of the creek, and his hand moved, soft as a bird's wing. His fingers kept stroking and she felt half-asleep. But of course they were not safe.

"Anyhow, a car too they could trace." He took a step away and looked up the steep banks. "So. There must be other methods, don't you think? See, these shades you brought—all that—would you recognize me with these on? And my cheeks stuffed to look fat? Isn't this a beard, more or less?"

But she could find no way to laugh back.

Again he pressed his hand along her hair. "So maybe I'll take the train." Why was he finding things so funny? None of it was funny. He picked up a white stone from the ground and turned it between his fingers. "You do see, don't you? You'd have to leave all this."

"So?"

"Your parents—you know how much it would hurt them? And your scholarship, your plans for your mind. No, it's no more horse fantasy—it's real." He had started to smile, but couldn't. "Very real." The desperation in his voice reminded her of the first days, how she had helped him, like a mother with a baby.

"Malca, where I'm going—or where I get put, probably—I wouldn't take an enemy. Besides, I'm no . . . " He shook his head. He was standing practically next to her, those thin lines beside his mouth only inches away. And suddenly she threw her arms around his neck; he did not stop her. A bit awkwardly, he held her, hands pressing against her back; they rocked from side to side.

"Dragon can find his way home." Her voice felt thick. "I'll help carry our food."

Under the overhang, Gavin's blanket-roll was tied and ready. Pulling away, he started toward it, limping with that lurching gait. "No." His voice was steady. "You're not giving up for me everything I've been forced to lose." He grabbed up his flashlight and the razor, working them and the food into the pack. "Here, I've been leaving lots of junk around, these last nights. Let them think the person long gone." His voice was flat and it took her a moment to realize what he meant, that he had started sleeping somewhere else. "Not far away," he added, gesturing beyond the thicket. He paused. "I wouldn't go far."

A paper, the map of the white summit lake, rolled out of the pack. She stooped to pick it up. Her fingers clung, trying to memorize the elevation lines, the peaks, the road and river.

"Don't." Gavin stood at her side. She let him take the map, roll it slowly.

"Malca." For a moment, he pressed her hands. "You do know. Besides, *you* they won't hurt. Though I am scared they may hound you."

"I'm not afraid." She lifted her head, chin up.

He touched her face. "But I am. Couldn't you tell, when I laughed?" His hands were shaking, and his thin body trembled—but not, she realized, from fear. It made her tremble, too. "Hold me," he was saying, in a funny way, and she did. Then something she never expected started, there where his left hand touched her cheek, and turned into a sweetness in her throat, a longing electric like night sky. Again his arms went around her, this time clutching tightly, and they stood together, lost in the silent woods.

After several minutes, Dragon lifted his head from a patch of grass and, snorting, pricked his ears toward Western Trail. Wrenching free, running to the stallion—he mustn't neigh and bring attention—she felt her body torn loose from what had become its home. A moment afterward, her own ears could make out the sounds, jinglings and stompings far down the trail but coming near.

No, not now. Turning her head, she saw Gavin crouch against the cliffside. A large round rock, white and grey, lay to the right of his feet. Sweat rolled from her armpits down her sides.

Then a child's voice mixed with the ragged clompings, and, a moment later, other voices rang out and someone shouted a command. Just a riding group, then, there beyond the woods. The hoofbeats rose along the trail, and, after another minute, fell into a rhythm of bumpy, jouncing trots. Steadily fading, they curved on, along the winding route toward North Meadow and Oaks Wood, and away.

Holding the horse had taken all her attention. "Too close," she whispered. But Gavin didn't answer. She turned. He was there again, right at her side, eyes watching her, but from some other place. The bedroll and pack were on his back.

"It is time," he said.

For a moment, she hugged him. And stood still, not moving except the trembling in her throat as their fingers held and slowly parted, letting him step away. *Go with God,* people said.

Halfway up the gully, he turned to look back. His expression was strange.

And then he was at the top, and then there was no one there, only a slight brushing sound moving swiftly, and a shimmer of light on a scarcely seen figure fading silently, with an awkward limp, down the sun-dappled path.

A fly buzzed nearby. Still fearing Dragon might neigh, she stroked the horse's nose. She pressed her face against his chestnut coat, but it felt alien, the vacant warmth of a pet. She looked beyond, up the gully. *Gavin, what did you see? Please be safe.* Nothing else mattered—now she would take every subterfuge, attempt no matter what, that he stay free. *No matter who you are.*

Carefully, her eyes searched the glade, scanned the broken tree branch where he'd hung the old canteen, peered along the overhang, the high dark boulder, the sheltering brush. She not only saw the wooded creekside, filling already with absence, but sought whatever traces other, hostile eyes might find. Gathering the few telltale scraps, she roughed the ground and strewed dead leaves across; then, lifting up the reins, she led Dragon through the water to the other bank.

"A GOOD JOB TODAY." GERILEE'S EYES TOOK IN THE COOLING HORSE. "I see you've learned to make him walk the last half mile. Smart you took your time. Real smart." The stable manager was looking hard as nails, standing on the bottom step below the tackroom door. "Your Daddy just called, and said would I drive you home. His friend Robert's got to advise you on the law." Gerilee's jaw clenched. "Like, I phoned your Daddy first, two–three hours back." *Not the quickest, but she cares about you,* Mom had said.

Malca tossed the reins to the young assistant, Dante, instead of herself leading Dragon in to get his brush-down. Gerilee took her by an arm and pulled her toward the stable's old white van.

"Hon, we better go the back road. James has been up to the Beltway again, few minutes ago. I'd intended he check where Eric went. But what James tells me, they're still gathering there—hanging out yonder, he says—trying to sober Eric up enough to guide them. Couple dozen of them."

Malca shook her head, eyes innocent. *No matter what.*

"Pigs, sister," said Gerilee. "Police."

Part 2. Trail Crest
(1971)

Gavin

For now, dryness *must* suffice. Deep in this storm drain, curved in its singular universe, of necessity the concrete forced a cramping of not only body but mind. In assurance of someday the moldy murk of it.

Two years back, when Navy guards had chased him down across the mud flats of Port Ruh, he had played heroics, "Go—run, Jason! Maura, Andy, run," taking the brunt and watching them—the *cadres*, as they called themselves for courage—flee along the white path, scale the fence to safety. He was the one who had got too involved, setting the mix congealed with sand into the twelve truck engines and those jeeps, and missed the guards' approach; therefore the loss had been his doing and he had to play it out, fighting back until he went down struggling, straddling the role as he had played before on playgrounds and the street—even when the damn Marines flung him hard across the hood of Port Ruh's sole patrol truck, pounding, "Boy, who're your fuck-ass fuckin' friends?"

Even then, it was not the physical fear had got him, not until this last—already close to two months ago—those shots while he stared into the halo around the streetlight, stupidly watching the frantic soldiers by the truck across the road. And it happened faster than a person could expect—as in a movie, the blue-white blast too soon, before he could even think, *But they can't still be living.* Then police lights pouring through the brush.

He had not connected these phenomena, too swift, yet sure that now they'd take him in—the heavy doors close down and his mind be locked apart from all consideration of the rhythmic paradox that might disarm the vicious counts, he had shredded the joint to slip away. But then stood rigid—hesitating, for any move could be the worst. So when no one called out "Stop," only that crazed "Hey you, hey you" as in a dream, he had turned, thankful for the miracle that he could walk away unhindered into the trees—and met the slashing agony. *Bullet, bullets*—in that moment, only the one simple thought. His feet had taken over, then—*Hey, Gav, you race so fast, that's great how fast you run!*—and carried him and carried him, even wounded they had carried him, into the woods and thickets and a meadow, down past muddy streams—hours he could not remember, except the running and then walking and finally crawling, until he could not move at all, until nothing, not arms nor legs, worked, unable even to drag him from the water, mind crying *Oh but the water can drown and the water is cold,* like a song.

Amazing feet. And he would do anything, a lot more than try to sleep in this rot-stinking drain, to get farther from D.C., and not to go through hell again. Yet he would have to. Somewhere sometime. *Nutcase Killer Pacifist Blows Ordnance.* "Gavin, suppose the cops really think it's you," she had said, meaning perhaps it was indeed coincidence, the truck so close. And if only he had gone instead to the hippies' tents, brought his guitar to start a jam or reminisce about Ricardo, stopped by Hamburger Patty's for a coffee, lost in a chord progression . . .

No, no point to such stories now, only to holding out.

'Cause in truth this world held worse than bullets. It had never been physical fear, or even Port Ruh and prison after, that had overwhelmed him. It had been the going home, straight from the cellblock to that two-room pad and Mama sick and moaning "Get out, get out, why are you here?" and all those calls to find his father's number and say "Man, she's lots worse—now you must come." It had been the discovery that every friend was fled or turned, the Movement gone to "counterculture" playtime or to violence, and a Vets for Peace guy the only man around who recognized his jail-hard wariness. The war kept widening, Mama worsened, and the numbers centered on Ricardo dead and women killed beside dead babies in straw huts, while he stayed on and lived. Until at last the substance of the whole had drowned him down into decision and the land of metal box-rooms and the rest, down to the truck and now this run that never—there was no point pretending—could end.

Therefore it was unquestionably better to have left Malca. She had thrown her bird-skinny arms around him in that gully. And, that moment, knowing what this was for her, he had thought to stay no matter if it meant to throw away whatever was left. "Who are you, what *are* you?" she kept asking, scared yet always coming back. For so long, there had been no one but her, with the delicate bones and that look that wasn't charity or compassion but raw empathy. *She has no safe place for herself.* And he had been frightened for her, there on the slick red clay, dropped into his world where no choice was right and the past only killed—where no one was safe however he tried.

In the dark, that gaze remained, steady when scared. She had saved him; she had not run; to hurt her was unimaginable. She did not even realize what was happening. *Anyone would love you, Malka, but I am half-again your age.* Therefore he had decided, in the way of the world, to make things clear before this could get worse. But gently. The only thing they had in common, except she liked the music, was that he too would have stopped to help, and returned, even fearing the stranger. So, having sung her songs and thinking then to comfort her while he said what would break her heart, along the damp grass he had clasped her soft thin hand. And felt it turn, quite helplessly, to press against his own.

If that had happened in a movie, it would have made him laugh. In this world, it felt like an explanation.

He stood up in the culvert's opening. That hand had been all clarity, slashing through blue darkness. "I am *no* victim," he had blabbed at her. As if it mattered. No one could know the rest.

Malca

It was nearly dark when Gerilee, taking backstreets, drove Malca home.

"Okay, hon," Gerilee said, squeezing her shoulder in a brief hard hug, and looked out the rearview mirror. "Be careful, hear."

In the driveway beside the house was a dark new-model car. In the living room, a grey-haired cop stood waiting with a warrant.

But it was the cop who was being questioned—by Robert, Dad's old college roommate. Robert had left physics, Dad had said once, to go into law and help people. The warrant called her a "secondary" suspect, but the cop just urged, "You should cooperate."

"You're due at the jail by Friday," Robert explained after the cop drove off, "but I'd say go tomorrow, get it over with. They'll arrest you—you'll be fingerprinted, you'll get your picture taken, but that's all. Don't worry, you'll never see the inside of a cell." He had hard blue eyes. "You plead not guilty, of course. Then we start bargaining."

Dad was all stiff around the mouth. "The thing is," Robert told him, "what've they got, the word of an alcoholic horse groom? That fool took two hours to even find the place."

She slipped around the end-table to the couch.

"Want a Pepsi, Bubbie?" Dad pretended to smile.

"Tell me, Malca." Robert peered at her. "Do you know where this fellow is?"

She shook her head. There were a hundred reasons Gavin might have taken the map of the lake.

"He never told you of anyone—a relative, maybe?" Dad was probing too, throat tight like he couldn't joke anymore, eyes huge with wanting to protect her. "A friend he might stay with?"

She must not say anything. But the pain escaped, desperate. "He hasn't—Daddy, he hasn't anyone!" Only, even those words could betray him.

"Well, good," Robert said. "Good, then it's easy. 'I don't know' should cover almost everything. You go right ahead and talk with them, Malca, you'll do fine."

She couldn't remember the title from French class, but the author had been Sartre, and in the play a prisoner saves his life by making up a place his friend is hiding, and then it turns out to be true. She shook her head and took a Pepsi. Condensation dripped down on her tee-shirt.

"Look, this guy's been in an institution. Anybody can mount him a good insanity defense." Robert cleared his throat. "You need to get your own life back on track."

Dad's eyes were brimming. "Bubbie, you have fine judgment, and I'm sure your friend's a decent lad. He wouldn't want you hurt by this."

She sat straight, the way the vigilers would. "You mean, I should turn on him?"

The old refrigerator hummed in the kitchen, the enameled clock that had been Granma's ticked, and some new kid was practicing a piano, poorly, down the block.

Mom stood against the stair rail, looking like the girl in hiding up in Sonja's attic. She was wearing her brown linen museum dress. "What I am thinking"—she stepped forward, holding out a dish of pretzels—"now what I am thinking is maybe it's time, Dan. Time we ask Malki what *she* would choose."

Dad wrinkled his forehead as if confronted by a stubborn math problem. Malca remembered telling Gavin, "No, my father's not in war research, just basic physics," and how Gavin burst out laughing.

"She's not even seventeen," Dad said.

"In October." Mom was pulling a cigarette pack from her pocket.

"You know I'm not happy about this?" When Dad paused, they could hear the piano going *twinkle twinkle, twinkle twinkle.* "But I guess you're the one now, Bubbie, has to make your own decisions."

There was a soft padding sound along the carpet, and Elvis, the old calico with the white and black whiskers who always slept outside, hopped up beside her on the couch. Malca stroked him, listening to his purr. She drew her finger down the can of Pepsi, and closed her eyes. "I will not cooperate. No."

Mom put the plate of pretzels on the coffee table. She smoothed her dress, and blinked. "Malki, your dad and I think you are showing more courage on this than an adult."

IT WASN'T COURAGE, THOUGH. OR THE RISK OF BEING QUESTIONED by men in suits and shaded glasses. It wasn't Hannah's "That was stupid," or Nina calling to say "Don't throw yourself away on a nutcase. Couldn't this be a substitute for rescuing your mom? My mother says that often happens in families." And it wasn't the neighbors' sidewise looks, as if she were some circus sideshow candidate, so that she wondered *Is this how it felt when they put you in the metal box?* It wasn't even the love underneath Dad's questioning, the terror for her in Mom's eyes. The refrigerator hummed, the couch lay warm and comfortable; nothing had changed, and none of it was real. The woods had been electric and, as he turned to flee, his eyes had been so strange.

After midnight, she stuffed her big denim purse with things she might need. She cut her hair, hiding the trimmings under some Kleenex in her trashcan, and plucked her eyebrows narrow. She took out the sixty-eight dollars from her desk drawer, put on two tee-shirts and a long skirt over her miniskirt to look heavier, and pulled back her hair with old-fashioned barrettes. Carrying her sandals, she sneaked past her parents' closed bedroom door, walking on tiptoe and avoiding squeaky boards, like Anne Frank in hiding (and Mom too, probably), and went downstairs. From a top shelf in the kitchen, she took $360 of Mom's "just in case" funds, barely running her fingertips over the small heartwood box where Granma once had kept the creased old photo of Grandpa Chaim with Mom and Aaron, and where now Mom kept Granma's locket and two rings.

Turning the front latch as carefully as when she and Hannah used to practice escaping from kidnappers, and pushing the purring Elvis back inside with her left foot, Malca slipped out. *I'm sorry, Mom. I'm sorry.*

The night sky had a pink tinge, the pallid light of the half-moon nearly hidden; the street was empty. If she could reach the Greyhound terminal, she could get a ticket to Scranton and change buses on the way. To throw them off the scent. *I'm too scared for this, I don't know how. And if he's killed those people–* But none of that had stopped her in the park.

Gavin

"Yeah, once I finish, man, it's P-H-D time. Otherwise, I'm primo draft material. Hey look, there's a buffalo. They're really comin' back." Wolf laughed, big namesake teeth gleaming in his suntanned, sweating face. "You never seen a buffalo before, I bet."

In the passenger seat, Gavin stroked the little mustache. It felt like sawdust and it wasn't growing right. At least the beard didn't itch. "Bup'hlo," he said flatly, nodding. "Cowboys and Ind'yans."

There had been close calls, or, in time's balance, nothing. The pregnant woman who kept staring, back there near St. Louis, in the gas station. The rumpled guy who ran out yelling, "Hey, hey stop," from the thrift store where he'd found the sleeping bag. A frowning cop, across the Mississippi River bridge.

Even so, once he had taken that first frightening step—because the trap was closing and it was necessity to risk the larger shooting gallery—there had been only the work, here within this bounded universe, of perfecting a thick and veiling accent. He had stuck out his thumb, there on the highway outside Rockville, thinking *Hitching's crazy, Gav, you're daring the white gods*, only the dumb Beatles-style shirt and office-jock sunglasses to keep him from playing target. Right away, that sporty woman with her don't-care style and the old white Volvo had given him a lift to Baltimore, the whole time recounting her travels through Morocco and fingering her slacks, and then the insurance fellow drove him halfway to Pittsburgh, lulled by classical music through the night. There must have been a score of others, each driving in a different universe, each a novel frame of systems that could never run parallel.

Yet at no time did it happen—*Now they're coming, now they shoot, look what you have done*—that whirlwind horror of the bullets.

Once, the girl had argued, "You are not a destructive person," the delicate straight eyebrows almost furrowing. "Nobody is, Gavin. It's thinking you are, that's what's destructive."

"You sound like a radical," he had said, so she had ducked her head and smiled back.

"You liked that buffalo?" Wolf said.

In the strange way of contingency, all these people loved to talk—those, at least, who dared risk picking up a dark-skinned foreigner, a bearded sunglassed stranger with a heavy, lurching limp. They liked to tell this ignorant alien what America was about. It felt weird. Not what they said, but just hearing people again, a voice not Malca's or his own. Every word seemed irreality; this was a different world, one that moved, full of changing persons, life that was not merely red-striped rain-wet walls. Almost, he could forget and it was fun—fun as in the commune years before Port Ruh, fun like the band or Laura—that was her name, the shy girl he had taken to watch an eclipse, there in time's observatory. Fun like living. He had forgotten.

"Bull knocked you speechless, man?" Wolf laughed.

"Diph'rent. So diph'rent." He couldn't do those rough "r"'s anymore. *I worked to get rid of my accent and now you want it, Gavie?* Ahmed had been laughing, that afternoon.

"Like, you'll see lotsa strange animals, out in Seattle. Whales—whales in the ocean, grizzlies in the mountains. That's a good school there."

Gavin remembered to stroke the mustache. "Is said to be."

"Better than this shit-trap I'm stuck in. Boise sucks for girls. Fifties pussy—look-don't-touch." Wolf took a gulp from his canteen. "Want some?" He passed it with one hand, the other gripping the wheel.

"T'hank you." It would be good, pure Scotch. Before, it sometimes drowned the count. Gavin shook his head. Always a trap. "You see, however, we do not d'rink 'this." Taking the bag of raisins from his pack, he pulled out a handful for Wolf. "So much big space here."

Somewhere beyond Laramie, near evening he climbed out into a strong south wind, and after standing on the empty road until the old Dodge disappeared, took off amid infinity, fast as his bad leg allowed, thrusting through the high prairie grass beside the highway. Always, the nights turned into strangeness and the obdurate choosing of some sheltered place where no dogs barked. He would have risked instead to sleep out on the open plain, daring what once obtained and might again, but thunderheads had gathered and, down the road, about three hundred feet beyond an old gray house and what might be a barn, a copse of aspen sheltered a low, white, narrow structure. Some sort of animal hutch. He slowed his pace and curved around to it.

After pulling on his gloves, he slowly pushed the plank door open, shutting it behind as quietly. Inside, the hutch was warm but dark; it had a weird smell, but one side held mesh panes like miniature windows, so at least he could breathe. Nothing stirred, in any event, and the mesh was weak, the windows tall enough; he could flee if chance required. The leg was numb now; soon it would throb. Stretching the sleeping bag across the tarp, remembering he had come here from some distant act, he half-fell onto the welcome bed.

An hour later, he knew, startled from sleep, that he was thirsty but it was something else had wakened him. He stared into the darkness, trying not to breathe. No sound. No one was out there, nothing. As he lay back, taking a shuddering breath, a package landed—no, some creature—hard upon his stomach, sudden as a kick. Not heavy—sharp. Before he could stop the mental count and move, another blow came, this time on his shoulder. Two pale things streaked out of the dark, hurtled past his face. Long flapping things. Ears. *Oh Jesus, rabbits.*

"Grrr," he hissed, "Grrr."

There was a rush, a scurrying. Two more of the rabbits hopped in front of him, bounded up onto a bale of something white, began to squeal. The metal pole they'd bumped against was swaying; then it steadied, swayed again, and fell. It struck a metal tub and clanged.

No more. All the rabbits now had started jumping. Someone in the gray house must have heard that clanging tub. A farmer, wakened, must be staggering to the phone, lifting out a shotgun, pulling on old boots. Police would come, fast and silent—the door would burst open. Bullets. Bullets entering.

Out. Reach the woods.

And afterward somehow reach Mexico. Find some last uncounted chance. Yet first the lake. He could wait there, deep inside this stricken universe.

Oh, and for what, Gav?

Never mind—only reach it. If he didn't turn into a lousy rabbit first, or get caught like a hunted mangy fox.

He lay rigid, knees to chest, then again jumped up to flee.

Malca

In the morning, she struggled over a sandy ridge and, passing a granite outcrop, reached the main route, High-Cross Trail, following its dip into a stand of aspens and up long switchbacks through the spruce. By midafternoon, still following the map, a topo map like Gavin's, of Mt. Intend and another ridge and, four miles beyond, White Pass—which he had called the "pass with the lake always partly iced, and snowflowers, and they say you can see past half the Rocky Mountains—it's a place I really, really want to see, Malca"—she came up, thinking to cross what looked like a rock-lined saddle, before an oncoming thunderstorm, and topped the rise.

It had all been too hard, like nightmares. "That's gone," Gavin had said of the hours after he was shot. "There are only pictures, like bits of film. I was in a meadow and I crawled toward some vines 'cause what if someone saw, but there couldn't have been black wolves, you know." Now she understood; there were only confusing slivers, single frames with the rest missing.

In the depot cafeteria in St. Louis, she had eaten a hotdog, head aching from sitting up in hot buses, and thought *I can't go on.* Her clothes had been sticky and itching and felt dirtier than ever in her life. The television was showing the morning news, and there were old pictures of Gavin and then her yearbook photo—but even her friends could never recognize her from that. And then the broadcast showed her father, saying "It isn't right, it's not good law, threatening an innocent child with jail"; and Mom, looking like coming out of the camps, said, "So if you see her, don't you squell"—meaning *squeal* or possibly *tell*—and blew smoke that floated toward the camera. *Wow, Mom,* she had thought, *That's impressive,* and the hotdog had fallen to the messy formica table. Mom must be hurting for her.

She had wanted to stand up, right then—to run and buy a ticket home. But she'd kept her face expressionless; too many people were around

That night or the next, when the bus stopped, long after midnight, outside a diner in a tiny Colorado town, she had risen to join the ten or so passengers getting off for a snack. The young Mexican woman sitting behind her, cradling a sleeping toddler, put a hand on her shoulder and pushed her back down onto the seat.

"No, sit yourself and I go get food. Stay—watch my boy." The dark eyes held hers. "Safer for you, yes? You like sandwich, french potatoes?"

Gavin had told her the sun was so hot, that first morning, that he had slid down into the creek, "But how could I have got across it?" He couldn't remember, and now she understood, because she could remember almost nothing about the blond-haired college student. At least, the blond man had said he was a college student. He had offered a lift, outside the camping store in Boulder where she'd bought the pack and sleeping bag. No buses headed out to North Wilderness, so she'd agreed. The man shared his root beer and chips, and played good music, but his hand kept bumping her knee when he shifted gears. Only, had his fingers actually slipped inside her tee-shirt? He had stuck his smelly tongue between her lips—or hadn't he? She couldn't remember, except pretending a stomachache and then really getting sick and him saying "Your farts stink" and finally letting her rush into the gas-station restroom. She had stayed a long time, ill at first and then waiting, like a creature in a burrow, hoping he would go away. But had there been other rides, or only the one long ride later with the old, taciturn truck driver? That man had been kind and let her sleep, her head against the high cab door.

What she kept remembering was the moment Gavin, reaching the gully's top, had glanced back, and the look in his eyes.

She took a hard breath, leaning down to tighten her right bootlace, which kept coming loose. Breathing on the steep climbs was easier now. The first night in the wilderness, she had barely dragged herself over a low rise, shoving her sleeping bag under a pine that straggled up from a crack. She had stayed awake, because in Rock Creek Park she had not believed—and at the stable been too slow to understand—that Eric was spying on her.

The first night on that rise, the world had been full of unknown thuds and chirrs. It had been black everywhere. *Anyone*, she had realized, could lurk out there. And Gavin . . . he changed so much, he was haunted by something all too real. No no, in the morning she could turn around, head home. Only, then she would never see him again. *I can't go home.* She had curled up tighter, shivering. *Remember his courage. Remember in the park I felt afraid.*

Late the next afternoon, high on a slope of aspens, she had bathed in a creek and stood in the sun to dry, awed to be standing there, alone in the silence, in wilderness. But each day the trail turned rougher, and yesterday she'd got lost. In the narrow shade of a red boulder, swatting mosquitoes and watching clouds build along a ridge to the south, she knew she could die here. But on riding camp treks they would always check for landmarks, and finally on her map she recognized the mountain to the left as twin-peaked Mt. Intend, with the seahorse-shaped Green Lake at its base. Marking the ground where she stood with an "X" of red stones, she started hiking forward. Two hours later, forcing herself to go on, she had reached Green Lake in its cirque below the double mountain, and in another hour come to the junction with the steep but wide and well-marked High-Cross Trail.

Now, giving the bootlace another pull, she straightened. Beyond the rise, the trail, still wide but rock-cluttered, dipped slightly, curving right, and rose another fifty feet. Sliding a little, she started forward, hurrying because the storm was getting close. At the crest, she stopped.

There, practically at her feet, crystalline and still, reflecting the clouds and a fading sliver of blue sky, lay a mirror-smooth lake rimmed by fragile grass and white-blue flowers. To north and south white slopes rose sharply, scattered with stunted junipers. Ahead and behind, distant peaks fell away. A jay cawed in the branches of a single pine, and twenty feet ahead two pale boulders rose, one a tapering pinnacle, the other low and wide.

But as she started forward over the rocky pitch, lightning flashed across the west. Trying not to panic, she turned and, slipping on the sand, rushed back along the trail and into the spruce below. Even as the storm crashed down, she crouched beneath the trees, removed her pack, and struggled to untie her tarp. There was no time to figure out some way to hang it as a tent. She wrapped the sleeping bag around her, pulled the pack against her lap, lashed the tarp tight around everything, and knelt there, hoping the taped-up cloth would hold, not leak. Her food was gone except two strips of jerky and a handful of nuts and raisins. The wind blew through like needles. *Your heart's in the right place, Malki, but you must be more careful, you must.* She tore off a piece of meat and chewed. *Mom,* she thought. "Songs in my head helped," Gavin had said, but she *could* not sing, cringing in the forest while the lightning crashed above.

SHE SPENT THE REST OF THE NIGHT PRETENDING THAT THE HUNGER gnawing in her stomach wasn't hers. By morning, the climb had become too steep, her boots too heavy to move. Maybe he had meant a different lake, or had not come this way, after all—she could have misunderstood. Exhausted, she could get hurt, here; another storm would come. *Go back while you can.*

A half-mile up the trail, she stumbled, tried to rise, and slipped back onto the rocky sand. Boulders slanted all around—squared-off and rough, black and red. She pulled out her map, trying to focus, and sprawled against a thin white snag, too worn out to keep on. *But you can hold back your fear.*

THE LAKE WAS TRANQUIL WHEN SHE TOPPED THE CREST. A SINGLE cloud reflected on the blue-green water, and the pale grass by the shore barely stirred. A jay flew up, its caw resounding, from the lonely pine; silver light gleamed, rimming the tree and those two stark boulders just ahead. And from behind the lower boulder a shape was rising, thin and dark. Cautious at first, then scrambling openly to the rocky platform, he stood, intently watching. His beard was full now, and he wore—it looked wonderful on him—a wide-brimmed hat.

"Gavin—" She stood there crying, her arms out as if coming home, and he jumped down, smiling like the boy in the newspaper photo, and ran toward her, the bad leg lumbering awkwardly at each step, across the stony sand.

"You found me!" "No one followed . . . " They did not finish, but held each other—as if there were no danger anywhere, as if the lake and granite mountains were the earth and the whole of time; crossing past the boulders, they turned, walking slowly, down the western slope.

Gavin

Were there some meaning to pray to, he would—would write a whole concerto in the piercing mode of gratitude—in thankfulness that she was safe. None of the rest mattered.

Merciful. Kindly compassion.

Malca

Five hundred feet below the pass, the forest thinned, on a sheltered slope far from any trail. Gavin's lair looked sturdy, nothing like the creekside shelter. A tent was strung between two young pines among house-sized boulders; a firepit was dug against an outcrop.

But she could no longer stand. He slung her pack from his shoulders, and she slid to the ground beside it and leaned against the tent wall. "I did get scared."

"I know, I know." He knelt beside her. He pulled her to his chest; she smelled his warm skin. "I saw a headline when I went for supplies. You are the bravest person. You are."

She shook her head. "No. I'm timid."

"Like an eagle." He gave her a smile so glad she felt the sky gleam. Even now, it cut to her heart, seeing that face again.

"Gavin, I thought—"

"So did I." Their hands clasped tightly, almost painfully.

"I was so frightened." She would tell him more soon.

His arms went around her. "*You* will be safe with me."

There was no storm that day, and sunset came with clear pink and purple light on the highest peaks. "I'm home," Malca said, without thinking, but Gavin held her wrists in silence.

THE WHOLE EVENING, HE HELD HER. BEFORE SHE FELL ASLEEP, HE showed her around the campsite; they kept stopping to embrace. He squeezed her hand and let it go, then jumped up on a slanting boulder. He laughed and suddenly leaped down again, staggering as he landed on his injured leg. Recovering, he began to spin her around by the waist. "We are here," he was saying. "We *are*."

Later, he led her back to the tent. On the way, they passed a rope between two branches. "For drying fish," he said, "if I can ever catch any." They passed the firepit, ringed with rocks; a hundred yards away, a gully dipped to the left, its hidden far end forming a latrine. To their right, beyond a stand of pines, a rock ledge climbed up to a cache he'd hung from a narrow overhang, two ropes dangling sparse provisions in a plastic sack. There was canned fish, he said, rice, dried fruit—"But I couldn't bring much." He jiggled the smaller sack. "I'm moving half of this upcreek by the cliff, spread the risk. Getting it meant going into stores." His voice wavered; then he grinned. "But possibly the beard worked. My accent too—'cause I fak-ed thisss ack'hsent." Lifting a hand, he pointed back toward the pass. "Those lakes up there, Malca!"

The words were ordinary; what she heard was his voice. He said, "I was so afraid for you."

They had reached the tent. A pond glinted through the pines, where a creek descended down the rocks, the water deep enough, he said, for bathing, "But when winter comes, this will all turn refrigerator. Anything around will starve. See, I saw an old cabin down-valley but it's fallen in, just slats. So I'm not so sure. Not—no, I don't think so." He broke off. "You didn't even eat, but you kept coming up that trail."

Too tired to stay upright, she lay back on the ground and heard him say that he would feed her, and touched his hand. Soon he was bringing rice, a tin of sardines, water. With his knife, he opened the sardines, careful not to spill the oil. Shaving twigs, he laughed, "Like boy scouts, huh?" and placed them in the firepit, laying two sticks across.

"If we run out of these"—he struck a match—"I have a flint. Not that I've ever used one."

It had been ten days. "For your sake," he said, just as he had the night before. "Better we don't." He crouched beside her on the sleeping bag. Beyond the tent's deep flap, bright moonlight filled the sky.

"I'm not scared, Gavin."

"Even so."

But, a moment before, his fingers had grazed her thigh, touching her in the way that had become, in these few days, her life, and she'd cried out, longing for him, pressing his whole hand against her skin. Only, he had lifted the hand and moved away.

Now, still crouching, his arms around one raised knee, again he avoided watching her, instead peering out at the night. "Listen to me—you are too young. Seriously. And now we have—now there is time for us."

It reminded her of a song. Reaching out, she touched his forehead, drew a hand across his eyelids.

"Don't you see?" he said. He shook his head. Her eyes misted over; her body felt softer, different.

Then he shifted, sliding closer. He began to smooth back her hair, the thin hot fingers stroking, over and over. Even as she watched, he leaned down toward her, a darkened softness in his eyes. His arms wrapped about her shoulders, and he lay still, tight against her.

Now she had to swallow; she could not speak.

In the narrow shaft of moonlight, he began to pull away. He made a strange deep groan.

"Oh Gavin, please—" Electric in helpless longing, she pressed against him, hands extended. "Gavin—" Lifting her chin, he searched her eyes. Taut and lithe, he stretched above her, eyes gleaming. But he seemed to wait, mind watchful, body asking *Are you sure?*

She tried to answer, but could only nod. He clasped her tighter, hands tender on her breasts, her abdomen, gaze never leaving hers; then, motions surging hot and swift, he sought her. Sought her—until, while the silver moonlight shifted, his body probed and entered, and they rose and fell within the sharpened sweet electric halo and slid down into that deepening place where no one was ever lonely or afraid and they had known each other since the start.

Gavin

These trees would be cold sentinels when the snows came—too hard a gift for that fragile innocence. This camp could only be a way-station

"Not likely they would search in Mexico," he had answered, even seeing the reality. She had replied, "Oh," voice strained.

Now, walking alone through the early morning toward the cache, thinking to bring her some present—even a piece of dried fruit, there still were three—he found he kept smiling. It was strange: he used to think having someone love him so much would drive him to fury, but instead all that mattered was to keep her safe. Obviously it helped that he knew how, here. When he was young, Ahmed had insisted they go camping, and in the course of time's count he had learned what was called woodscraft. Not much, of course; instead—hoping to discover galaxies—he would rush to grab the six-inch telescope with its EdiStar mount and, leaving Ahmed alone to construct their fire and set up the tent, go observe for hours over the lakes.

Yet he had failed in observation of the closer mystery, those years that Mama never came along. "I must rehearse, you understand," she would say and hug him as if never to let go. It was sentimental to forget there had already been the shadows. Shadows and silence since long before memory, sucking down their life. Something had happened—the massacre his father spoke of, fingering the filigree, but something else too. Something, perhaps, between them. Silence hid that.

Silence had muffled the darkness underneath the Calvert Bridge, no fire crackling but those guys already dying. He had lifted one foot but not stepped forward—not until it was he hurting.

Enough—this was prehistoric news, those cut-off screams, cut-off lives. Clearly, what must count, at last, was what remained. And, today again he was letting Malca stay—using up the delicate life, then becoming impatient because she still feared him.

No, screw all that. There were hard tasks ahead, whatever the direction, whatever had once happened in whatever count. And if he knew too much, still further paradox arose, and none of it resolved, bags of ideological garbage. He had rehearsed this stuff too often and the crux remained—at what point violence turns to murder, murder to massacre, to war. The acceptable ration of dead to saved, the recognition that arithmetic like this could have no meaning, for each person was a universe, and so on—the usual. He knew this stuff, knew it by heart, and the goddamn scene from Dostoievski's Grand Inquisitor—*of course* he could imagine being that little girl locked for the night in an outbuilding, "and what if you could save all humankind by sacrificing this one child?" But Jason, hauling himself up the chainlink fence around Port Ruh, had answered, gasping, "Yeah, and if *not* sacrificing her means ten thousand kids killed by napalm?" At which, Annie piped up, "Violence can't change anybody's views," blah-blah, as if some sort of clock. And so on, even during that action which demanded silence. Like his mind's whir in the damp tent while he stared for hours counting the bright, lethal wires. Thinking, *Yes, I may.*

Now he pulled taut the rope, drew the bag up from the crack. For long stretches of reality, these arguments had turned to nonsense, concepts twisted to mere bundled words. Because he had seen his mother's suffering, a drain upon his universe yet a fellow creature pleading for an end to pain. And because he had watched the army truck pass underneath the Calvert Bridge each Monday night, traveling the wide road barely sixty feet outside his tent, bearing soldiers already primed to kill. Because shreds of dead people were to flash across the night. Because he had not moved. In the end, decision was the greatest trial.

He took the tiny pack of dried fruit from the sack and shook two shriveled apricots into his hand. Something better for Malca. The freshness of morning was complete, the air dampened by the foaming creek. He was glad she was with him, here, to know this beauty. When you are close to someone, when she is every moment's wonder, you wish to share your world, your soul.

And that, for everything and what might come, was his penance—the burden of the things she must not know. What he had not said about his mother's death, the facts of the soldiers' dying. His diagrams and careful devices that the public defender barely got suppressed during the Port Ruh trial. What had been forced in those metal boxes. What nobody must know.

In the scroll of the years, it could be argued, this was over. Or not.

He rose to his feet on the long grey boulder, looked toward the falls, and threw the hunk of wood that he had finished whittling far into the pines. It was supposed to be a horse, mane thick like Dragon's, a present, but it didn't work, it was a mess, too carelessly composed, the head and body all different widths.

Malca

From here on the scree line, the dripping trees by the tent below were full of raindrops in the rising sun. She felt so softened, her body—my womb, she thought—feeling filled by him as through the night before—as in so many nights, now. *Oh love.*

"But really, what do you do, the rest of the time, up in those mountains?" Nina might ask someday. And "We fish, we make traps for birds," she might answer—though not what it was like to catch one, hearing it squeal in terror, or about the hunger and how happily they'd eaten up the pika that they'd caught one morning stealing rice. Or about the night when something in the food had made her sick so she crawled out the tent so Gavin wouldn't smell her vomit, but he'd followed and held her, comforting her, in the dark. Or how hard it was to build a cookfire, or how she'd tried to air the sweaty sleeping bag. How futile it felt to forget her math and French and know she would lose her scholarship—how futile, for them both, to know the war kept going and they could do nothing, here, against it.

And how she missed hot water, and Mom, and even her pink bedroom, even Hannah's constant arguments, and Elvis-cat like a cougar prowling Dad's big chair as if to roam cliff-sided mountains, and how she sometimes thought *I really can't keep on with this,* but then the light would change or Gavin come to find her.

She stretched the washed socks and underpants across a drying rock, anchoring them with stones. It was warm here in the early light after the night's storm, and she stretched out her feet, resting a hand against the narrow trunk of a little pine. To her right, diagonal ledges rose toward a peak between their campsite and White Lake, but just ahead the land fell sharply down into a shallow canyon where a stream cascaded, the rocky depths twilit though sunlight already struck the treetops and upper pools. Gavin was down there; she could see him hovering above a shallow eddy, thin hands poised on his makeshift fishing rod. He was bent over, bad leg thrust sideways, to not cast a shadow that would scare off any lurking fish. "I'll go alone," he'd said, like he had about setting traps, with a flash of irritation when she asked, "Alone?" He had been by the stream since before dawn, waiting with that silly patience she used to find so amazing. She watched him move up-canyon, keeping to the rock, and crouch by a higher pond. At times, he was like a whole new person here, playful, singing with joy. Her eyes filmed, seeing how the light now curved along his cheekbones and the muscles of his arms. She wanted to reach across the rim and touch him. Every minute, she wanted to touch him.

No, not every minute. Sometimes she had to be alone. She would listen to the forest, inhaling its sharply cool air, learning its new sounds. The one like traffic was the wind, the thuds were falling cones, the cracklings were ground squirrels and tiny things, after three weeks no longer scary.

There had been so much else that she—they both—had to learn. Twice, looking for lakes to fish, they had been lost, but now they knew the routes across the boulders; they knew when clouds were only threatening but probably didn't mean storms. And sometimes their traps worked. The birds were small, and they worried what might crawl among the feathers, but Gavin used his knife to clean them, and last week he had shown her how. The first time she cleaned a whole bird, "Yes, Malca," he had cried, "Yes!" his hurt leg slipping terribly as he swung their hands back and forth. And there were times he could catch two or three trout, though most days there was not enough to eat.

But it was only after they had finished dinner and he had cleaned the knife and pot that they would rest, pressing close. Then sometimes he would sing.

She sang too, now. One evening he had stopped in the middle of a song and said, voice quiet, words precise, "I am not a record player. This is not some entertainment." A moment later, he'd apologized, the way he did. Once they'd been arguing about nonviolence and he'd nearly snarled, "'Oh, only one dead,' that's the way they count. How can there be such a count, since every person is a world?" Then he'd said, calmly, "We can try to reach them."

"If meanwhile they're shooting?" She'd asked it automatically, and he'd smiled and swung her hand in his. He could never stay angry long.

She knew that, now. She'd learned so much of what he was like. The way sometimes he acted like he thought he was no good, and at other times would laugh like a happy little boy. The way he'd speak of simple things like trying to rehang the tent, but then turn empty-eyed and barely move. And how, two times, he'd swung his fists against a tree and stood there shaking, as if he fought with something lost.

But also she knew what it was to touch him, yearning in the morning or the evening, and how their bodies found each other like the notes of some warm song; she knew the way they both went silent when there was no food.

All this, she'd learned, and also what it was to live with fear. She rubbed her fingertips along the bark of the little pine, not a young tree but stunted by the wind. Being afraid made no sense now, she could not still fear Gavin, and yet sometimes she did. Like those long hours when he'd say, too quietly, "Leave me alone"—or, worse, say nothing—and stare with rock-hard eyes, lips making their silent mumble while his gaze avoided hers. Last night, for hours she had lain awake beside his sleeping form and waited for she didn't know what. They were so alone here, and she was ignorant, as he was not, of how to stay alive in these wide mountains. And it might not be those people killed, it might not be his own dead, but something—whatever it was he'd never said—still emptied his eyes. Less often now, but, when it happened, sudden.

But even darker was the other fear—the one they both lived with, hearts pounding at any sound that shouldn't be there. Someone could have recognized her in Cincinnati, in the motel with the green-and-yellow neon sign. Or the college student, or those pacifists she'd met in Boulder, or the trucker, a bus driver—someone could have guessed. She had recognized Gavin right away even with the beard, and he'd told her that, the second time he'd risked a trip down-mountain for supplies, a woman in the little roadside store had looked afraid. "Of my limp, possibly—it scares people, like something weird toppling toward them—or she may have figured things out." The camp was hidden and they hiked, most evenings, up to the lake to scan the High-Cross trail. But it was "a matter of time," as he said one night. "You may find this a vacation, some days—I cannot." He had been trembling, so she held him as hard as she could.

And when she was frightened, he held her, even those times when it still was he that scared her.

But most the time, especially like now when the work was finished for awhile, and everywhere the pine needles shone like mirrors, and the tiny half-dried flowers gleamed in shallow soil between the rocks, and Gavin—tired, carrying only the fishing pole and his journal with its dangling pencil—came toward her, turning his limp into a glide, and put his hand against her face, and neither of them could move except into the other's touch, then no one, she thought, could ever have been so glad.

"LOOK AT THIS," HE SAID. THEY MUST HAVE BEEN RESTING AFTERWARD, lying close, watching the shadows change. Now he was holding out the narrow, blood-marked journal. Once it had been his mother's, but by now half the pages were in his own writing, an almost illegible, up-and-down scribble. He had jotted all sorts of things, but mostly theories and some of his remembered songs. These last few days, she knew, he had been writing new songs.

"To sing?" She felt sleepy from the sun.

"No." He was holding the book open at the very first page. "Just look. I decided I want you to see this."

She rolled over onto her stomach. Pulling herself awake, she took the volume. As she read, she pressed warm against him and leaned toward the pages to make out his mother's small letters. "Your mom was very bright," she said after awhile, and felt him nod. Near the end, she asked, "Do you hate her, Gavin?" and he said, "Not usually, not anymore. She was just a broken, sick little lady in a trap."

There weren't many entries. "I was in first grade there," he said, pointing to the first one, "when she stopped doing ballet."

The entry began like a cry. "Not so! 'Not so,' I told Doctor Graeb, 'I've never heard of this, this sclerosis.' All night afterward, Ahmed wanted to hold me. How could I say, 'Oh don't, for God's sake. I just want to dance. This has nothing to do with you.'"

The next entry, two pages written a full year later, had a title, "Finding Joy in Ordinary Things." There were more like that, short essays, attempts to be hopeful. Gavin was studying her left hand, or the hairs there. "You wanted to know stuff," he said, voice muffled.

"That unlikeable child"–this entry was underlined. Another, from the years his father was away, was called "Finding Meaning." It could have been interesting, she thought, if the woman could stop complaining; only, words like "demands" and "unbearable" kept leaping out. Two entries were prayers; another began, "Ahmed is back, loyal sheepdog," and another, "soon our sole/soul miracle." But Malca barely saw them. A few pages further on, huge shaky letters sprawled like black spiders into the margins. She squeezed her eyes shut.

"You want to trust me, and you won't read the rest?" Again he sounded irritable. She jerked her eyes open. And there were the last, scrawled words, "Dear God, if any, let the boy help. And protect him."

Sitting up, Gavin bent over, studying her ankles. "At home," he asked carefully, "did you actually shave your legs?"

"Not often." She tried to remember. *Protect the boy.* Mothers were supposed to do the protecting.

Protect Malca, Mom must be thinking, waiting beside the worry-gate. She had to let Mom and Dad know. It *was* important to take care of parents. *I'm happy here–don't worry.* They didn't need to know she was afraid. Afraid when that distance took him, when his brow clenched and he only saw . . . whatever he had done. She said, "Why did you shave your beard?"

"It was only to get here with, obviously. I hate beards." He touched his chin. "You know, everything in this diary, it was Ahmed should have been there. I hated him for that, for leaving. One day, the sensible shrink—I told you, that guy Williams in the metal joint—he said, 'But your mother wouldn't have wanted him around, would she?' And I guess Ahmed knew that." He looked up. "That's what it was." He had taken her hand and was swinging it.

"What?"

"What I was thinking—tripping on, rather, 'cause I was too stoned to think—that I didn't hate my father and his mumbling anymore, and that I only wanted no one to hurt again." He swallowed, fingers pressing her palm. "You remember what we argued about once, whether it could make any sense, killing someone to stop a war? It was this I had decided, that night—no, recognized that I had decided—watching the streetlight."

FREEZING, SHE WOKE, HORRIFIED THAT MOM——ONLY, NOT MOM but Granma—had rushed in from the hallway and was bouncing on her stomach, crying "Where is Malki, where *is* she?" Mom just stood there by the doorway, saying "Malki, you are *much* too ravenous these days, and also on cold nights we keep the windows shut." But a person had hopped onto the windowsill, a girl who was really Sonja, saying *You are truly queen now, Malka. Never cease to dance or you will lose the castle.*

Her eyes jerked open. An ice-thin light of the waning moon had slipped in through the tent flap, the white glow pulling her, but in the cold she huddled, seeking Gavin's warmth. Why wasn't he there?

Then she saw the dark shape, awkward like a tall clumsy bird, dart across the rocky ground between the tent and pond. Its legs thumped twice, to some unheard beat, and leaped—to land, weight jerking sharply to one side, thrusting. And leaped again.

She squeezed out through the flap, hurrying, frosted air making gooseflesh on her naked skin. Out there, he too was naked, dancing backward like a ghostly negative in half-light, darkness pallid in the moon.

"You're cold," he called, hands stretched toward her. Shivering, teeth chattering, she took three frozen steps across the sand; pine needles kept sticking to her soles. His arms reached out; his warmth surrounded her. "Here, here," Gavin laughed.

A moment later, he had taken her hands to whirl her around. She saw the treetops spin and the stars curved like the trails in old astronomy magazines; Gavin was humming a song. Then, chanting something in a language she didn't know, he was leading her in swift sharp turns and running circles, almost like the Israeli dances back at riding camp.

"I am not surprised," he said, when she told him, "'cause all those countries are connected." They kept dancing, faster and faster, though his leg slipped twice—their breath coming quick, their feet stamping hard, and even if the world was cold with coming winter, they were warm, silver in the moonlight.

Gavin

"In extremis, our limitations demonstrate themselves." He did not know where he had heard those words, some time before that blue light. He had been living then, for months, down by the bridges in his leaky tent, bailing rain and listening to the cars, the songs no longer coming forth from his guitar. It was hot and sweaty and boring, and he could not escape the images—the mouth in the dead face, a hand reaching out toward a switch in the metal-box building, Ricardo rotted in some Far East swamp, a puppy he had once seen crushed beneath a car. Lying on a torn blue sheet, nursing an occasional joint, he would read the papers, old images merging with the photographs, "Soldiers Take Out Fifty Cong," "Thousands Die in New Attack." He knew the quandaries and the arguments by heart, Gene's "What if the fellow's finger's on the Bomb?" and Annie's "Suppose they shoot at somebody you love?" but it only grew more urgent, time and the war closing in. *By comparison*—his mind again rehearsed the arguments, freed of rhythmd composition—*by comparison*, one wrist slit, one small family's dead, was nothing; it was all a computation issue. Yet if no one person's life could count, then neither could the millions; the universe itself must count for nothing. Then he would think, *No, this is crap, more of that goddamn maze*, and would light another joint, glance over at the little pistol in its waterproof case beside the bundled wires, thinking again *mind-fucks, garbage*. Because it kept on—how to stop the war, how to save anyone when everyone had left . . .

Sure, Gav, the way you saved your own folks? Like a joke, the thought had jerked him up, awake in the dank June evening, into more pink-tinged smog. Knowing the issue determined, he had silently lifted the tent flap and carefully crawled outside, looking past the bushes toward the waiting road. The truck was there, halted.

Precisely—except the swaying of the blue-tinged branches, and the long, long knowledge he could by simple decision strike that blow against the war—the way he had told Malca.

Malca

In barely another two weeks, the last flowers disappeared, the birds took flight, and the grasses everywhere turned brown with fall. That night, the storm had not let up—the soughing in the pines, the lightning over the pass, the chilling rain. "It's coming," he said, cradling her against the cold. "Winter in the mountains. Soon it's time." Time to go down-valley, he must mean, but there they'd be dangerously close to two towns. She held him tight.

In the morning, as they moved about the dripping camp and huddled in the tent, she caught his tension. It wasn't just being crowded in; it wasn't only fear. Last week, he'd seen "some late-season backpackers" far from any trail, scarcely two hundred yards above them and heading cross-country over the scree. "They didn't notice a thing," he'd kept repeating. "They were making for the pass." But since then the heaviness had taken over—taken over as it hadn't since the park.

By late afternoon when the sun broke through, he was shifting every minute, pacing like a caged wolf, breathing sharply under the closed-in tent. She watched him fidget with the narrow flap. Those eyes looked out as if his heart was frozen. When he stalked outside, she made herself follow.

THE CLOUDS HAD CLEARED, EXCEPT A DARK LINE TO THE EAST. LIGHT clung on the ridges, gilded and barred through the woods. He was mumbling almost silently, staring toward the pass, but this time she could make out words, and the old tune "In the pines, in the pines."

She tried to laugh. "We *are* in the pines."

He didn't move. He leaned against a granite slab, back turned to her, and something in that stance, the tension in his roughened breathng, and his hard stare as he'd stalked outside, gave warning. Throat gone tight, she halted. Only, this was *Gavin,* she could trust him; she knew it all the way down to her toes. He could be so funny, so good a person. Even after those backpackers, he kept making up Shakespeare lines when she got sad, to make her laugh.

"Bespeak, wench," he said now. But in a tone like knives. He still didn't turn. His hands kept pressing on a dead black fir.

"I—" Her words wouldn't come. And when they did, they poured out, too fast, not at all what she'd meant to say. "No, Gavin, Gavin, listen, you have to tell them."

Shoulders hunched, he pressed the dead tree harder, as if he'd make it break.

"You *must.*" She couldn't stop herself. "Just say it wasn't you. Please, Gavin. And you can get a lawyer. Or"—she imagined rifles, men in wide hats spreading out around a cabin—"we can leave. We have to. Let's get away, we can get to Mexico—they'll kill you here, this way. And we are fighting all the time, we're not—"

"Oh, shut up." He turned, half-slipping as his weight fell on the injured leg. Again his lips moved as if praying. "*Dear.* Remember, I have told you. People, you lock them together, can turn enemies." His fists clenched. "Life goes dark upon this universe. Do not make yourself my enemy."

"You think I could ever be your enemy?"

"I don't go to them. Ever." His mouth twisted. His forehead furrowed, eyebrows squeezed into an ugly *V*; it was an ugliness she'd seen before. One afternoon beneath the dogwoods, he had played with a stone and said, *Oh yes. Oh yes, I helped.*

No one was near, no one for miles. He had taken one step closer, lips again moving—counting. Or was it prayer? Better she ask nothing.

But at his hard-breathed "Ever," voice strange and forehead creased into that lowering *V*—and under the looming *something* always present, sucking him into emptiness—her fear crescendoed. *Hers,* now, not mere terrors gleaned from newscasts or Mom, but fear of what forever turned his words to contradiction and his eyes to stone. And it remounted, here in the solitude, until she could not stop. "It's not just police, then, is it? Gavin, there *is* something—what?"

His mouth opened slowly. He laughed.

"Make sense," she said. "Make sense."

"I do. You haven't learned."

But they kept shifting, all his meanings, scudding like the sudden storms across these mountain passes. "Please," she said.

He blinked. And then his gaze pierced out. It wasn't angry, wasn't even laughing; it was glistening, like the warmth of sunbeams through the forest at the end of winter. The fingers of his hands clasped over her wrists. "Malca."

The word made her glance up.

Around his eyes, the skin was crinkling. His lips curved higher, and a smile spread. "Malca, can you still think I'm that idiot bomber? That I would try to stop a war by blowing people skyhigh?" His hands let go and lifted, waving back and forth before her face. "These could have chopped you up, blown you to bits, a hundred times while you lay sleeping by my side. They haven't. Obviously." He pulled her down beside him onto a rotting, moss-slicked log. The bark squished loudly, wet against her jeans.

"All right." Abruptly he loosed his grip. He sat, head bent. "All right, then—of course. There is something, yes. You sensed it, and you were right."

He wasn't touching her. She could stay, or leave.

"All right, I'll tell you, Malca. But you listen. And do not forget you asked."

Boughs brushed overhead. No storm anymore, but the clouds were already regathering, thick with heavy snow.

Eyes closed, he sat silent, like someone hearing secrets. When he spoke, his words at first seemed casual. "You remember that diary? 'Cause after awhile, all the lights out those windows turned dusty green, and the landlord kept ringing. And Mama no longer cared about anything, and if I even breathed it bugged her, 'Get out, you get out.' I stayed on the streets, mostly. And it's weird, I made good friends, street folks; I had two good years—music, protests, Port Ruh. But after that, after I left prison, the Movement was gone, everyone was scared off—and by then somebody really had to help Mama. She couldn't do anything but lie there, twitching and hurting.

"I would take her to the clinic—hours, you had to wait. That was when I finally tried to call Ahmed. He had moved to Cincinnati.

The phone number didn't work. I think that was his way of saying he only ruined things—like me." He glanced toward the pond, its surface reflecting the darkening sky. "They would not give her enough medication, and she did not know how to force them. But I knew the streets. Enough to help." Picking up a long twig, he began to draw a line upon the ground. "Sure, I helped. One night, I went down to Southeast and I got what she needed. 'Cause I knew what she wanted. Wasn't I—in fact—the expert on that?"

She reached over, trying to touch his hands.

He pulled away. "Oh yes, 'suspicious circumstances.' There's one killing we can all agree who did. I knew she wanted to die."

"Gavin—"

"Understand." With the twig, he dug a shallow hole. "This is only how it started. That night, I came in early. I brought back a little bag. Black leather, with tiny red pills inside. I put it on the floor, next to her bed, right beside the radio, and then I brought in a pitcher of water—it was a big glass pitcher—and she said, 'Thank you, Gavie.' I said, 'Goodnight.' I didn't know what else to say." He kept turning the twig, jabbing it against the sand. "She started to answer, 'Goodnight.' And then she said, 'Please.' After all, I was over twenty-one, I could help as an adult. So I did. I held the pills, while Mama held—at first, Mama held—the water. At some point, she said, 'Forgive me'; I wish she hadn't said that. Each pill I'd lift, she swallowed. Until she couldn't. I was thinking should I call an ambulance. Her hand, at one point, jerked up, but I told myself it was simply reflex. But suppose not? 'Cause it was too late—it might be worse if they could still save her. And she had wanted this." He shoved the twig hard, and it snapped, the far end falling onto the pine needles. "There might still be time. I went out to the park, until morning.

"See, suppose she did not really want to die? And there were times I'd wanted her to. You get awfully tired of it, the whole mess. The old woman always there, snarling and hurting. And the smells. I did not want her dead—but, Malca, I longed to be free. Of everything. In a way, it was I who wanted to die."

She had slid up close against his back, and now she huddled there, as if still to hold him warm. *This* was the emptiness, then, the reason he could not come back into the world. But in his words was also everything that she had sensed, these months, so that she'd never felt quite safe. It made no sense to fear him now; only, how could he have done such a thing? He must have had to lift each pill and place it—carefully, he would have had to place it carefully—on his mother's tongue. And then go out and leave her.

Just walked away. No, someone who could do that . . . he might do anything at all. He might be lying, even now, about the bombing. He might be anyone. Here there was only the emptiness; nobody was near, nobody. Tomorrow she must flee, she had to. She must be careful, say only *I was wrong. I was wrong, dear love, this isn't me, I cannot stay with you.*

Except . . . She pressed her nose deep in the rumpled wool of his sweater, damp with the odor of pine needles. His mama had had to beg to make him help her die. Otherwise, he wouldn't have, ever. Because he was himself—he was Gavin. He hadn't even stopped to think what it would do to him, just given all he was. She pressed the wool against her face, breathing him in. She knew him.

The darkened forest was silent, only a rattling of dry leaves. Somewhere far off, a bird called, left behind with autumn.

Her throat felt tight, her tongue so heavy it hurt. She tried to speak, but couldn't. He was curled over with his face down on his knees, back rounded and eyes hidden, like a child.

"But don't you see?" He raised his head. "I killed a universe." Even in the twilight, his eyes gleamed. "I've asked myself so many times, what if she changed her mind? Yet what if I'd refused?" The words were a cry. "No, even if someone were in agony, I . . . See, this is what I understood, that night in the park—there is nothing anymore could make me take a person's life. Not anyone's." He straightened and sat still, hands hanging. "Well, I guess that's extreme. Clearly."

There were no other sounds, only a pinecone falling from a tree beyond the tent, and the humming wind. After awhile, "You wanted to know about that truck," he said. "Do you, still? Understand, when I saw those guys blown up, and that woman out there—she seemed to lift her hand but she too was dead—I did nothing. Not anymore, not after Mama. But also because they were hurting, or they were dead, and I was them and it was too late. And this—and you *know* this, Malca, you *know*—what had just happened was exactly as I had devised. Because you know what I'd been thinking—glad to believe I might truly *strike a blow* against the war—that very day? *Oh fuckit, bomb the friggin' truck.*"

He laughed, that broken laugh she'd come to know. "Then I got shot. It's almost silly, isn't it?"

In the gathering darkness, she made out tears along his cheeks. There could be no other answer, no other question. Only him, only who he was.

"Oh Gavin," she said, "Gavin, Gavin."

Crouching, he turned. He stretched his arms around her, holding *her* now from the cold. "But for how long?"

"I'm here, Gavin."

"I really am the sinking ship, you know. That 'doomed rat' stuff. These months, I've had to learn it, but I didn't want you to."

"We've managed. So far."

"But if you had not stayed . . ." He scanned the shadowed scree. "You are my starlight—well, actually my universe."

Their fingers held. They could hear each other's heartbeats.

In the night, those black eyes were her universe; to him, she understood, she was the universe. Yearning. *Merging our hearts.* He had covered her hands; he lifted them above their heads, a bird against the sky. With one finger, he traced an arc along her palm. Everything was there.

"This is our love," he said. "Remember this."

In the dark, the world flew on. No further answers. "Gavin," she repeated, "Gavin." *As you'll say when he's dead*—the thought, like the earlier image of rifles, came from nowhere.

"What's wrong?"

"I *am* afraid. Not of you."

Gavin

Uncountable, in this time the stars must freeze all darkness.

He felt her stir, warm at his side.

"I will protect you, you know?" he said. What counted was here, this softness. He sat up, daring the chill. "Sometimes I want to live so much. And I can, Malca, but only if I fight them."

Those slim fingers squeezed his wrists. All around them hung the welcoming silence and the solitary chir-chir of a late-season bird. Bird calls—yet wasn't that how enemies signaled, in old movies? Now Malca was stretching, her arms extended, sleepy. He ran a finger along her hair, holding back the truth. "That poor bird's starving. We, too, should have left, by now."

No, no point to hiding it. "Come morning, we need to start down-valley."

She had clutched his hand and was pressing her face against his palm. "I'm with you, Gavin."

And, sucking in his breath in fierce happiness, forgetting the rest, he pulled her close.

Malca

"What I did, what I almost did." In the predawn chill, he lay there in the sleeping bag, lips pressed together and eyes half-shut. "They will always pull on me."

She shivered. They should leave right now, not lie around worrying. She dragged herself up. But it was far too cold; heaping both their sweaters over her shoulders, she sat crosslegged atop the bag and shivered; she looked down at his face all puffy from some dream. He didn't seem to see her. "Let me tell you something," she said finally. "I knew. Last night, I knew."

"Yes, I realize that." Was he being sarcastic? "It makes me truly glad."

"I don't mean just trusting you. I mean . . . Gavin, I've never known anyone did more than you, trying to save everybody. Your mom, your whole family, even those soldiers." He had to understand, not look away like this, lips making that soundless motion. "What I mean is, you are trying right now, you're still trying. I mean, it's this, what 'pulls on' you. Like down to death. I mean"—she forced out the words—"this going back and going back to save them. Even dead ones. To bring them home safe, you know? You *are* the person in your song."

"Absolutely." Flinging himself over, he hunched in the sleeping bag, nearly dumping her off. "Now you're a shrink, Malca?" The words came muffled by the thick down. "Killing is 'saving,' right? Keep 'em from suffering, all that? Sure. Think I've never considered those sophisms?"

It was hopeless, but she had to tell him. More than life felt at stake. "It's true. You did want to save your mom from that suffering."

"Obviously. So would anyone. It is called euthanasia."

"Those guys, too." She mustn't let him stop her. "The ones in the truck. And Vietnamese people. Like in your song—just like in your song."

"Malca, stop poking at it."

Half-turned away, he lay not moving a muscle. But there was something in his posture, something in his tone, that didn't quite fit the cutting words. And finally, mostly curious, she leaned over and pulled back the edge of the sleeping bag that covered his face.

Out of the corner of one eye, he was looking back at her, and one hand pressed the worn cloth of the bag as if he touched a precious thing. His lips opened wide, like a little boy's, in a helpless smile. "I guess it is true," he said slowly. "What you said, you know? About saving people. Yes—yes, it's like the song."

THERE WOULD HAVE BEEN TIME THEN, IF THEY PACKED QUICKLY— now she was sure of it—time enough before nightfall to reach Icy Lakes to the north, or a sheltered creekside down-valley. But when she'd returned with water from the pond, he was sitting in the tent entrance, the other sweater over his shoulders, whittling. And, except "Why run in circles?" and "Okay, this changes everything, okay? So let me think," practically all he would say was "None of this is so fucking sure."

Now, "It's already freezing," she attempted, shifting her weight on the flat rock. "We'd better leave soon—we can get a little way, before the snow."

"It'll melt." Across the firepit, he kept stirring the beans and rice around the deep pot with a stick—not a meal to quickly cook. "We're not the Donner Party."

"I'm not panicking."

Grain by grain, he pinched a bit of salt into the bubbling stew, and stirred. Precisely, carefully. There seemed no other motion anywhere, as if the forest floor, the boulders, everything awaited winter.

"Yes, all right—yes!" Of a sudden, he dropped the stick and leaped onto a narrow boulder. Arcing his right arm wide, he hurled a white rock down the wooded slope. "All right, I *am* postponing things. All right, so now it's time. So let us deal with it."

She felt a shiver, something trembling up her back—but not the old fear. Rather, it was the knowledge, certain and hard as these rocky peaks, that he was about to wipe out her world.

"No, I am not so sure," he said. "Not sure at all where we should go."

"That cabin?" But her head felt empty; she remembered the big hats of the men with rifles in the dream.

"That cabin is boards by now. Mice. Filth." He was stroking the boulder, gazing at the tiny clearing. "This has been our home."

"Yes." Even to think of leaving hurt. She pressed her hand to the grass beside the rock—quickly, because the gesture seemed absurd.

"Malca, what I said last night, about when there is hope?" He stepped nearer and sat on a peeling log. "The only way back for me is to keep fighting them." He pulled at the hanging bark. "This hiding like hunted animals is not enough. And there must be a few people left who don't believe I've gone maniac; I only need a few. Not to go bombing with, or something, obviously—but not just chopping out a jeep or two, either, anymore." He tossed the loose bark toward the embers and stared at his injured leg. "Do you *remember*? Malca, if they ever did this to you, I would . . ."

"Why are you saying this now?"

He put out a hand, not quite touching her. With the other, he traced what had been that long red wound. "They've put me there already, you know—there, in that role. Imagine what they'll do when I truly take it on. 'Cause I have to. But you do not."

"I can fight." She squeezed her hands into fists.

Again he started to touch her. "Last night, I understood what I must do. And what you said, this morning—there in the tent, you know—about me being such a person!" Lifting the stick from the pot, he pointed it toward the ground. "See, I've been going around on that all day. Here into infinity. 'Cause it is infinity—we are not simply a count. We are each infinity, Malca—but with centers, and each center reaches out." This time, he did touch her, for a moment held her wrist. "Now everything is ready. Everything." With the point of the stick, he began to draw a map along the sandy soil. "There must be somewhere we could go together—but that too is theory. And I will not risk you."

No, she had to stop this.

"Another thing," he was saying, "you are starving here. I've seen how you watch the food. I even wonder . . . Never mind; in the morning we'll head down past Five Creeks—today, if we hurry. We can take the old track north." He began tracing the map, detailing a route. "Here, see? And in three days we come out to the highway. There's a store, a half-mile off, may have a phone." He tossed the stick down on the sand. "Though I'm not sure who we call. Those pacifists in Boulder, maybe, those Quakers you made friends with. Would one of them drive up?"

"I didn't 'make friends.' They were painting picket signs and I started helping. Then we leafletted. One of the women knows Amanda."

"Amanda? From that vigil?"

The women had all been very polite, extremely friendly. "I didn't say anything. I changed the subject."

"Good. Good, then let's risk it."

"And then? After they get us into Boulder?" But she knew.

"Get *you* into Boulder." The muscles in his neck moved, swallowing. "Please, stay with those good people, if you can. 'Cause I really don't want you getting arrested."

He thought he was protecting her.

"Another thing." His voice became a whisper. "If something happens, don't—see, I want to have been good for you—don't let it haunt you, please. I want you to go on."

She understood. The world was closing; he was closing it. "You can't just dump me."

"Me, too, you know?" Again he swallowed. "This hurts me, too."

Where will you go? But she did not ask; if they must separate, better she not know this.

"I get so scared when I think there is hope." His hands moved back and forth again, apologetic. "Scared of this foxhunt. Especially now, with the fox worth saving."

She bowed her head. *Yes, that much is done. But then save him, Gavin. Save him now.*

Too slowly, he was rubbing his heels through the sand, blotting out the map. "You know what you have given me."

She remembered how people at the vigil spoke of hope. There were a few faded stems of flowers, what Gavin had guessed were penstemon, to the left of her boots. "You too," she said. "You too—what you've given me, I mean."

"I kept hoping we—" He looked up. "I've put you at too much risk."

"Gavin."

But he had turned and was limping toward the ledges by the waterfall, to bring back what remained of their provisions for the long trip out. So little, almost nothing, it couldn't take him long. *But let's just leave.*

Only, the time for fear was past. She dragged the pot out onto a cold slab and hurried to gather up their few extra clothes.

Gavin

Of course there must be no delay. Yet, in the new sequential mode of time, there had been real necessity to think through this new truth. To reach past all counts to clarity.

No matter—any move was too great risk. Too late. Sing, choir: *too late.*

From where he stood above the crevice and the cache, he glanced back toward the tent. Malca was pulling something out, her neck smoothly curved. Those slim legs were well-muscled now, her carriage a young woman's, no longer a horse-crazy girl's. Still fighting fear with courage, but each time more swiftly, still shy but no longer so unsure—ready to shape her own path through the world.

And finally she trusted him. That she could, even after what he had told her, felt like the world opening. He could barely believe his happiness, here in this pine-shaded universe, since that moment in the dawn—since her quick brief remark, seeming at first pure psychobabble, "You're still going back to save them. I've never known anybody try so much to save people."

It had taken too long before he understood—watching the soup rise and fall as he stirred, back and forth like his own familiar dance with death, *run run* but refusing to save himself and instead, counts entangled with the songs, reaching to save the people or, strands turning taut, to hold together his reality. And when at last he comprehended that those words she struggled forth, shaking with brave fragility, were simply true and all that he had done or grieved for came from caring, he could not keep back the smiles, silly as that first silly grin this early morning—kept smiling here on this ledge even now while he lashed thin cloths around the dull dried lake-fish and, tying swift knots, secured them to the pole. Those shrinks had spoken what might seem the same words, there among the metal walls, of course—but as something to be cured of. But she *knew*. She knew him.

To bring back the dead. As if he climbed a chasm with the ocean pouring below, gripping the slippery rock sides to bear the people out, time after time, and always struggling not to stay under, not to hang in the wave, but to lift each person and himself to safety. As the tiny girl had dragged him up the bank.

And, frightened but holding back the drowning, she had understood. Yet never had she stood, unmoving, in the blasting blue glare and known *I could as easily have caused this*—then failed to do what might, past what was counted possible, yet save. She had never placed into a palsied mouth the little red pills, never opened the door in the morning to find the dead. There were times he had imagined each half-rotted body like a stillborn puppy's, saying wordlessly *I was the universe. If you had died, this void would now be yours not mine.* His mother, lips gaping open and arms spread out as if inviting someone home, had lain like meat, the rigid eye-jelly under heavy lids explaining *You couldn't help in the right way.* The soldiers' bodies had been blown in bleeding pieces like steak sandwiches, the woman flattened to a pallid slab.

But if Malca had not seen death, she had recognized love. And this morning she had said, "You more than anyone, Gavin—Gavin, that person's you!" Meaning, someone who risked going under to do what must be done.

And must again—for himself now, as well as for the people running fugitive beneath the bombs. If those millions dead were to have meaning, so must any single life. He had known this—understood how thoroughly he knew this—watching those two poor frantic soldiers as they struggled with that truck. *There in the ghetto,* she would argue, *people learned they must shoot back,* but the lessons of his own flesh were different—never again to take the route that killed. Yet his route now must be serious, daring the circus edge of violence. *Where, love, indeed I will not risk you.*

Certainly she could be kept safe somewhere. And some day he would find her, and bring new songs no longer so haunted; there could be a future.

Except—already the light was slanting yellow, ripples on the water turning bronze—none of it was so damn sure.

For it had been safe here, a place to grow whole, and today—in this new knowledge, deeper than paradox—to hope. *You are such a person!* He straightened, tied the cords, lifted the pole. The count was stilled.

They could take this game path—easy, really—down the slope. Over there beside the alders, they could cut across, follow the creek through the woods into that little meadow. There, the trees ended abruptly, in a curving row ringed by heathery grass and thistle. With the rising breeze, the late-afternoon light shone through the fluttering tufts, turning them to round haloes of many colors. One was actually white. Unless it was a feather from a bird's wing—perhaps an osprey's? No, it was triangular.

He lowered the staff carefully, guiding the packets onto the moss. His breathing turned shallow, the stiff thudding of his bad leg more than a nuisance. As best he could, he loped through the thick pines' long shadows, seeing again their rhythms. *For how do we count / and then why shall we count / for each life counts / each one . . .* His lips again moved, swift and silent. At the forest rim, the thistles—ever more silver-and-purple, up close—spread around him. The white triangle lay, clear against the soil, among dry cones and needles. It was about three inches long, and not quite triangular but slightly crumpled. He picked it up between two fingers, feeling the gritty softened paper. There were no words, only the blue lines of a notebook, a mark that might once have been the numeral "2". Smudged now by dirt or water—impossible to know how recently it had fallen or been torn.

No more than two miles could be possible, this late. Those backpackers might have been carrying writing paper. Or someone innocently passing, perhaps some camper they had failed to see. Rushing through the night in panic would be worst; they could fall into whatever they fled.

The black dog lunged from the park's darkness, attacking the wounded leg over and over until he kicked the creature off among the vines and slid across a stone-block wall, slippery with his own blood. He had forgotten that, and the siren biting from the night, headlights bearing down until he rolled from the embankment into nothing known.

Run, Malca, run.

No. Whatever innocence depended on him must forever count as infinite. Because it mattered, mattered without end.

The paper could be something accidentally fallen months ago and somehow sheltered from the rain.

Malca

She had not waited long but it seemed forever, the fire doused and their sweaters and socks folded in a backpack with the towel and socks and the menstrual rags she hadn't even had to use, but Gavin was not back. Already, the light glowed red and gold, a gaudy sunset scattering long beams along the forest and changing all the peaks into uncanny beacons. Following the deer track back around the boulders, she headed through the pines beyond the pool and crossed the glistening shale.

A quarter-mile up the path, she saw him standing on the pyramidal outcrop where the creek cascaded from the lake above. Here, where the notch of the pass was most visible, he was peering toward the distant trail beyond the rocks that leaned together like a jagged balustrade.

She climbed the steep-slanting granite.

Turning, he limped toward her, holding out a hand. His eyes were shaded. Carefully he began, with one finger, to trace the line of her brows. "At least there's a little while."

She couldn't speak. It felt as if they were memorizing each other.

So quietly she barely heard, he said, "You are the most wonderful." But that was silly; he was who was wonderful—he, and this, all this. She lifted his hands to kiss them.

The shadow of the crests had not yet climbed up from the valley. Here, in the strange gilded sunset light that poured in through the pink clouds piled from north to south below the circle of blue sky, it was as if a gate of the universe were opening.

"Like the New Year," she whispered, remembering Granma going off to services she didn't believe in—but frightened because gates also close. "Like blessings."

"Blessings."

Below, the forest darkened. In the evening wind, they shivered, but stood still, not wanting to go down. Much later they lay, bodies entwined, in the familiar tent, and Gavin half-sang "universe" so they laughed, eyes wet.

"WE ARE TOGETHER?" SHE SAID THE WORDS TOO QUIETLY, SOMETIME after midnight, coming up from the silent happiness, trying to quell the new fear, unforeseen.

He turned in the sleeping bag and pulled her close; they rocked each other. She had really been asking—they both knew it—that other universe. The world of fragile blessings. Like babies, they breathed together.

"Shhsh." He sat up in the pitch-dark tent. Outside, there had been, perhaps, a sound. Like a little cat possibly, or a coyote, over by the boulders near the firepit. "Cougar?" she whispered—she'd been wanting to see one—and then she also heard it. But on the other side.

Gavin was slipping her shirt onto her, faster than she thought possible, and silently he was pulling on his jeans. Trembling, she began to slide into hers. He leaned over toward their boots.

And stopped. Everything stopped—only his sigh. All around them, tiny snaps and muffled crunches and other, stealthier sounds were approaching from behind the boulders, coming out of the dark pines. There wasn't anywhere to go.

"We'd best not scare them, then," he said. She reached for him. His face, shrouded by the darkness, felt haggard, like an old man's. He squeezed her close, and breathed against her hair and touched her cheek, and for an instant they clung, hearts beating. Then together they opened the flap in the side of the tent.

"Out, fast!" The loudspeaker blasted from the forest and flashlight beams struck their eyes. "You're under arrest. Throw down your arms." Malca, knees wobbling, couldn't stop thinking it sounded silly.

"You are surrounded." It was hard to hear, for the static. "*Don't make a move.*"

Her eyes found Gavin's, black and clear as the predawn stillness, to her right. Their hands were clasped. And to her left, out of the very corner of her vision, something, a heavy glinting thing, was lowering—

the muzzle of a rifle, maybe eight feet away. In front and to the right, guns pointed, cocked and senseless, at their heads. The rifle made a clicking sound as its safety was released. "Oh, don't," she groaned, mouth shaking.

Then something slid across her vision—Gavin, flinging himself, shirtless and barefoot, between her and the guns. His back was to her, and she saw him half-trip as his bad leg slid, then recover and stagger a short step forward. He was quick, quick as when he'd leaped awake the other morning, laughing, when she brought in pinecones for his birthday. Then, too, his arms had been stretched wide.

Only, this time his sudden swiftness and outlifted arms—and the jagged lurching of that thrusting limp, hurtling him sidewise and then forward in the flickering darkness—must have appeared a threat.

IN THE COLD OF EARLY MORNING, THEY WERE MOVING OUT—THE big sheriff Arthur first, on horseback—heading upward through the pines. Behind him walked the others, the tall trainee Ward and the one who had shot, followed by the sick mare Kentuck, packsaddle laden with the green plastic bag that held the stiffening corpse.

Malca, hands still cuffed, was placed behind the mare, and a deputy walked to either side so she couldn't lie down to freeze. Just behind rode the short lieutenant—"Schmidt," he'd introduced himself earlier, watching her carefully while the men drank coffee by the firepit, "F.B.I." Now he straddled a little half-Arab, scribbling what he called a press release. "You'll need this," he shouted ahead to Arthur, "if that *Free Underground* piece gets around." Malca's eyes turned, focused on the newspaper that Schmidt waved in his fur-gloved hands, "Truck Bomb, What Truck Bomb? How our army blew its cover(-up) in Washington."

The wind was colder already, hard snow coming down fast, so the men began to hurry, making quick time through the woods but floundering on the steep stretch toward the top. "Move it along," Arthur snapped, waving his cowboy hat like somebody swatting flies. "Over that hump before we get snowed in." Near the summit, where the ground began to ease and flatten out, he shouted again, forcing everyone, humans and horses alike, into a jiggling trot. Barely seeing the shrouded lake, its two lonely boulders lost in mist, Malca struggled not to fall.

The path turned sharply downward through the thickening snow, steepening as the switchbacks shortened to a rocky, straight descent into the distant spruce. Inside the metal cuffs, her wrists were swelling, and a blister throbbed beneath her twisted socks. Ahead, the sick mare's stained rump and swaying packframe filled the center of her vision, and to either side the heavy sack poked sharply forth in jagged, grotesque angles, as if its contents had been frozen in the act of fighting to get out. But the voice she clung to now sang simply, beautiful as any she had known, "We'll build tomorrow / free of wrong's horrors," his music merging with her granma's half-remembered "Never say for us there's no tomorrow," the forest and the ghetto fighters' song.

Only songs, though; this *was* tomorrow, each unreal moment sinking under layers of snow. He had been alive and now he wasn't; it made no sense, and never had. And in this world the cold hail pellets banged like bullets striking metal on the crackling plastic, swirling out of emptiness that hid all but the closest frozen footholds, while she held the pointless new life safe and warm inside and tried to recognize the way.

Part 3. The Hole in Time

1. Malca Bernovski-Cohn, 2001

Because Human Housing's newest outreach worker was a militant vegetarian and two of the social services staff couldn't tolerate milk, and anyway just in case, she had ordered hummus and pita, lentil-potato soup, and two mushroom pies, along with olives and crudités. She was alternating spears of carrot and broccoli, taste-testing the soy-berry yogurt, and trying to imagine ways to ease this meeting— though the task seemed hopeless, morning after Labor Day, affordable housing on the city cutting block and everyone frantically busy. She must set an encouraging mood, show the planned "direct method" in the best possible light, encourage every potential source, and so she concentrated, setting the final table arrangement and asking Marti, her admin-assist, which staff would actually help with the lobbying down at Waterfront, and was meanwhile lowering the overhead halogens a fraction more, when Ellen the receptionist, her wind-coiffed hair a bit awry, said, "Ms. Bernovski-Cohn, there's an urgent on line two."

"Urgent?" Clients always argued urgency—usually all too rightly. Malca straightened. "Sorry, just take the number, please."

"I tried. She said, 'Hell no, I've waited thirty years.'"

Malca lowered the olives tray and stretched an impatient hand to the phone. But somebody, one of the special projects guys, was entering the room already, and behind him the city attorney, so she ducked toward the inner door, saying "Ellie, hey, I'll take it in the cube."

Once inside, the single, splotchy window looked toward Golden Gate Bridge, but the view was narrow, only half the span visible between two glass-walled skyscrapers, and the room was claustrophic, metal desk with its old HP filling most the space. Irritably, she waited. Voices pounded through the wallboard, the activists and city people arguing. She picked up on the second ring. "Malca here," she sighed.

"Malca Bernovski?" The voice, a young woman's, had a frail sound.

She leaned forward, disoriented. This wasn't vertigo. "My maiden name, yes."

"From Washington, D.C.?"

Nearly fifteen years' experience in nonprofit administration had given Bernovski-Cohn a reputation for cutting to the chase. "May 12th," she said, voice breaking. "1972."

A seagull circled, out there between the skyscrapers, trying to find its way back to the ocean, and briefly there was silence in the room beyond the wall. This once, maybe the hole through time was real.

The woman across the line began to cry. "Yes, my birthday. Well, of course you'd know."

2. Malca, 2001

It was strangely hot. Gavin must have put their sweaters over the sleeping bag, trying to be protective and keep her warm, but even so . . . She touched his shoulder. Really, the heat didn't matter, though, only that she was here with him and the nightmare hadn't happened. She pressed her face against his neck and lifted the edge of the sleeping bag. It felt so thin, like a sheet—but of course that couldn't be, unless he'd got one somehow, which would be wonderful. "Gavin," she began, and sat up, leaning a hand on the soft ground—too soft, as if there had been rain; the air too seemed damper, warmer.

She lifted her hand, feeling for moisture on the tent-cloth, hoping there was no leak, that they would not have to clamber outside in the night, and hearing again his breathing. Her fingers stretched farther.

And touched something cold and flat. *What have you done?* she thought, but this was something slick against her hand. Like a cliff, vertical and solid, the wall beside the bed.

Blue eyes half-opened in the semidarkness, peering into hers. Quietly so as not to wake the kids, Jeff asked, "Your ghost?" He was pushing off the coverlet, and sat still before he rose to his feet. Leaning over, he picked up his pillow. He would carry it down to the living room; he would sleep there on the couch; she knew already. She recognized what was happening; it had happened before, a long time ago, and at first she had been grateful.

But later in their marriage, when all her attempts at "Let's talk about it, please, let's—" ran into his refusals, those hard years when the boys were going to preschool and Jeff still worked nights helping immigration clients, he had begun instead to lie there and ignore her. These latter years, he would instead turn over and go back to sleep, leaving her staring, bereft, one hand on the wall, touching her other reality. The rare times he would talk, she would be happy, ready for the struggle with him, the return to this world. "Yes, I know you can love both that ghost and me," he would say, but then not even hear her answer. But she needed to answer—to believe she could stop his drift into what surely must be self-indulgent jealousy, some obvious simplistic re-imagination of their marriage. Sometimes she thought it must all come from him—of a piece with his shift, these passing years, into a more remunerative form of law.

Well, she had tried, and so had Jeff, each silencing fear for the other's sake. Truly—and from this trying had grown, she often believed, real love and understanding that could endure whatever their divergencies, and for which no gratitude to any god or fortune could ever suffice.

And yet none of it could do any good. Because neither Jeff nor his increasing doubts of Gavin's innocence—indeed, of anybody's innocence—were what undermined the world. What still undercut the very universe was rather that *here* was where all this was happening, here on this side of the unbreachable wall, here in this wrong world.

Except, from a world, one could imagine traveling. This was temporality, the wrong time, the after-time. There was a science fiction story she had once read, about political dissidents exiled to an Earth before prehistory, so that return was not even conceptually possible.

Malca pressed her hand along the painted surface, recalling the touch of Gavin's shoulder, that touch she had felt only a moment ago. She heard her own breathing, smelled the dust from yesterday's smog. Barefoot, she threw back the sheet and crossed the white rug, passing the desk and the wornout oak dresser with its sagging upper drawer. She stood at the wide west window, fingers pushing back the curtains, spread out along the panes. Glass, wood frames—the bounds of this room, the eastern hills, the silhouette of San Francisco over the Bay—each formed a wall. And each walled her here because none did; nothing in this or any world was the true wall, the wall of time, with, even in thought, no way through.

I'm forty-six; I'm twice as old as he was then.

THEN. WHEN, AFTER THE WORLD ENDED——ALL WRONG BECAUSE THERE had been no point—and the hole went through between his mouth and where the back of his head had been, they put him in a plastic bag. A few hours later, while she pleaded that they take him out, the bag was strapped onto a packhorse, a mare who seemed too sick. During the three-day march to a county road, in the warmer air as they descended, or perhaps from the little animal's own heat, the odor began. It was slight, but she was positioned next in line on the long trek down. Each night, they would uncuff her, try to feed her, and let her "go wash" behind a tree—and, when they retired, cuff her again and zip her into a sleeping bag. In the morning, they reversed the routine. The third day, toward evening they jogged, past trees dripping in thaw, to the dirt-and-gravel road. Television cameras glittered, and there were lights and more police, in the background two dark trucks. A woman in a gray-green uniform took her behind a boulder and frisked her, first through her clothes. Afterward, a man photographed her face, saying "Watch the birdie." They loosed her hands for fingerprints and put on new cuffs. "Okay, get in," someone said, and another woman pulled her by a shoulder toward the smaller, green-blue truck. Before the door shut, someone clambered in to link the handcuffs to a bench along one wall and make her sit.

Rising to her knees, Malca managed to peer out through the tiny slatted window near the roof. And that was when she saw the green bag being hauled down from the mare. The ground was muddy but half-frozen. Two older men, one with a dark flannel shirt and sheepskin jacket, bent to lift the bag, and heaved it through the open doors of the larger truck. They slammed the doors and moved away—she couldn't see where.

Those doors had no windows; that truck was black and entirely closed, a metal can. Her dirty clothes and blistered feet, and the horror all confused with the odor she had trudged through, ended then. Instead, there was this other world.

This was also when the sound began. For four nights and three days, it continued—someone screaming; she could hear the voice and wonder who had understood so well. During her processing into the Denver "facility," and in the cell that night, the scream kept on, though the women on the other bunks warned, "You shut up, girl, you gonna get us all locked down—stay cool." The whole way back to D.C. on the prison flight, it went on, now with words: "No, let him out—no metal box. No, let him out—no metal box. Don't put him in a metal box."

"That's what we all get, sweets," one guard, a huge woman always out of breath, said, trying to be kind. A girl in the Denver cell, not much older than she, had said, "They kill yo' man, those pigs," and stroked her hair, but then the barred cell door turned into the truck's metal walls.

The screams were weaker, like a chant, early in the morning in the hallway of the D.C. jail. Her father was gazing at her with that awful loving pity in his eyes, the way he had in the living room with Robert, back in the other time. A matron was putting a bag of clothes and shoes into her hand and pointing to a restroom, saying "You freshen up for your daddy."

These were clothes from *before*. She had moaned. Then her father was folding her in his arms and whispering in her ear, "Bubbie, come on out of here without a fuss. You know what my parents had to do to get your charges lowered? Use common sense, for once."

Oh no, not the Bernovski money! Her mother's old line. As if all that were still real. "And my Tennessee grandparents," she had said to Gavin, trying to assure him she would not be jailed, so he would flee on time, before . . . But already the big sheriff Arthur and his men must have been close. Tracks, there would have been tracks in the snow; already there could have been no escape.

On the ride home with her father, she stared out the car windows, hearing the fading chant and watching what was no city she knew but only silhouettes under wavy glass, a grey world no longer the real one because there was none.

"It doesn't matter to him now." Her father glanced toward her across the gap, then back at the rush-hour traffic. "None of it—he doesn't know. Your friend died thinking to protect you—that's what counts, Bubbie. It's how we live that matters."

Remembering to let her father open the door, she climbed from the car and started up the walk. Only when she saw her mother toss away a cigarette, holding open the screen in rigid helplessness, did the words come. "Gavin died," Malca said.

She felt her mother's hand on her shoulder, heard the quiet "Governments, governments," and stood dry-eyed. Surreptitiously, with the backs of her fingers Malca pressed her abdomen in new protectiveness. *I will have him this child.*

3. Julie, 2001

What that woman told me on the phone came down to love amazingly strong getting lost amid a nearly equal grief. What she told me was that one condition of probation was she must "return to normal life and usual scholarly pursuits," and that, had she been incarcerated, I could have been forced into foster care. "Although my parents would have stepped in to raise you," she added; she said they were very supportive.

That beautiful, wonderful woman. My *mother*.

Well, birthmother. She doesn't like the term, but I can live with it.

I explained all this to Bill, but he hardly seemed to hear. He sort of glanced up from painting the kitchen cabinets, turning them the tint of warm mustard-yellow we thought we wanted when we realized how dark the condo was. But finally he nodded—and sometimes that's all he does but he's hearing me—so I sat down on a stool, sat right down there next to him, sharing that glorious breathable mix of San Jose industrial and homespread paint, and I kept on talking.

She said her parents already loved me and I was their first grandchild and I "meant so much to them." She said her dad's parents had pulled strings already and would again if necessary, probably, though "it wasn't sure." So it might seem, she said, the obvious answer would in fact have been for her to take her parents' help, to live at home and continue in school with her mother helping care for me—but she decided no. What if all these parent-figures were too confusing to the baby? What if in a decade or two she hated the child (me!) or the child hated her and felt deprived of a normal upbringing? I think really she saw the arrangement as a make-do, a façade that would deprive her and Gavin's beautiful daughter, their miraculous, frighteningly vulnerable baby, of that two-parent, perfect, loving home she believed adoption would mean.

That's what she has told me. I can't know what was true, obviously, but I know she was sincere. And most important, she told me finally, was the other thing—there it was: she was crying all the time. She would cry and she would go through these incessant thoughts—hope struggling to overcome her grieving, love for me (and for him) holding her, barely, over the great deep whirlpool that sucked and lunged to pull her down, "even as its depths—crystal depths," she said, "like the White Summit Lake your dad loved"—reflected her unended love for him—for us.

This is what she told me. Her words. And that there I was and I was there and she loved me and she was with me, protecting me and holding me, in her womb and then in her arms, before my birth and as I was born and for a few weeks after, but also she was other-where. She said this.

"For years," she told me, "I called it 'other-where.'"

And I found this strange, too strange to tell to anyone. Because, for so many years when I was a child and I would be, say, up in my room at night playing with my toy-horse collection under the dormer, or being princess of New Island or the Silver Countries, where I would imagine my "first parents" lived, that's what I used to call it, *other-where*.

You know what she told me? She said the world had been real and then it wasn't—or rather, she was not in the real world, she was locked in a world "after life." That was *her* other-where—or one of her other-wheres. One must have been the reciprocal of mine. Or perhaps they are the same world? The same time-universe? Hey, this stuff gets manic! But her loss must feel, I think, like how I used to feel, those nights.

"You ask questions so abstract they have no answers," Bill said, the sort of thing he usually says when he's working on a fix-it project or he's had a long day's work and thinks I haven't. "How do you expect me to know what you mean?"

So, "Come on," I laughed.

I do that; I play the decent-person card; I say, "What I teach is abstract. What you teach is worthwhile." Because of course to be a carpenter—even one knowledgeable in structural engineering—is, however honorable, not the same as a professorship. I struggle to minimize the status card—unless exceedingly upset; otherwise, I jeopardize our, and also Gabey's, well-being. I will not do that to Gabey or to Bill. Damn, sometimes he understands without one word.

OH MY GOD! I HAVE SPOKEN TO MY FIRST-MOM. SHE IS THERE. REAL.

Actually, my birthmom, she said a lot of things. She says I was the "airlock" between her worlds.

4. Malca, 1971

The way back. She had to find the way back. There was no pink light in the tent, but now she woke to something pink and sharp—reflections from the walls. Sounds, too, that *Eine Kleine Nachtmusick* thing, and voices, Mom's and Dad's, rose through the heating duct by her bed.

"Remember how it was with Mamelah, 'Where's Chaim, where's Chaim?' I don't want that for Malki," Mom was saying, and—sudden, loud—Dad answered, "After what he did to her, *I'd* shoot him, if I could," and then Mom's murmur faded as they moved off farther from the kitchen duct below, its thin slats like the bamboo bars of tiger cages in Saigon or the thin, barred grating of that prison truck.

Black, windowless, the other truck had rolled down the littered gravel. Something had darkened the earth where they lowered the bag from the mare. "Oh, don't!" she had cried, seeing the guns outside the tent, barrels glinting even in the night—but what if she'd stayed silent? Even if they'd shot her, even if they'd made him spend his life locked in a jail—

She must get back there, to that universe—back past this pretense. Reach through time to change it—to return to life, return Gavin to life. She pulled the sheet up to her neck.

"Coffee, Malki?" Mom stood in the doorway. She wore a black dress, simple and elegant, and carried two cups of coffee on an aqua-enameled tray.

Malca sat up, pushing away the linen sheet and pillow. The same sheet and pillow, with the white silky edging, as before.

That was his term, "before."

Mom lay the tray on the bedside table, handed her one of the coffees, and, balancing the other, sat down on the mattress. "Careful, Malki, that cup is hot. You know, when your grandpa died, Granma still had me to care for—and no way to. I have told you. People knew what the Germans planned. We had half a room, in what had been someone's fine apartment. Everyone was secretly glad, now another person gone—we had more space, more chance to use the toilet, to lie down. Every night, Granma cried Chaim's name—quietly, to let everybody sleep. Then Aaron visited to tell us goodbye, and we went across to Sonja's attic."

And Sonja? It didn't matter now.

Mom took a sip of sweetened coffee. Her eyes had that look of elsewhere. "They say the best guess is Sonja was among their hostages, one pretty Sunday morning . . . their White Christmas. Ten hostages—they were led to a courtyard. What you hear after so long is perhaps not true, but I would know if Sonja lived—there are organizations. Mamelah tried for years but we learned nothing. You do know that Sonja's name was Sonja-Mashenska? One reason for your own. They were good friends, her and Mamelah, from working in the archives; they thought the attic over Sonja's kitchen—above her stove, just under the roof—might be safe. But too hot, much too hot. We could not breathe well, your Granma and me, up there. We came down the ladder for air. Twice."

This did not matter, either. Except it did.

"I will tell you, Malki. Mamelah was lifting me down. The ladder ended maybe five feet over the floor—it seemed so high—there by the stove. Sonja had pretty ornaments, leopard statues, ceramic eggs, a glass shepherd, all the way across her cabinet; I always wanted to touch them. The chair with the red plush seat—it was kept almost under our trapdoor, and Mamelah stood on it, helping me down. I saw her face below me, very irritated—understand, we were both overhotted, stuffed together—and then her eyes turned, looking sidewise, and so did Sonja's—and four men came through the door. In dark uniforms, holding guns."

They had worn dark uniforms, lifted their guns.

Her mother set down her coffee cup. Its white china reflected on the maple table. The silver-plated teaspoon came from a hotel in Victoria.

"You are a widow now." Mom sounded like someone who'd been considering something. "Your dad and I have spoken. You understand, he feels this too. In our house, you—and he, your late husband—will be honored." Mom sniffed slightly. "And your child."

The bouncing light made ripples on the wood grain. An ant on the table could get lost but would never fall off.

Mom was nodding. "My first thought," she said, "was, this love made you look soft"—she must mean *softened*—"but see how you move."

Malca could feel her own tiny smile.

That evening, when her father got home from work, they insisted she come down to the living room. He sat in his big chair, science journals around his feet. Mom stood beside him.

"Now we rend garments," Mom said. "Malki, like this—you make a little cut at the neckline, then you pull. Yes, pull. Good. We rend garments and mourn."

TEARING THE CLOTH MADE THE CHANTING TURN LOW, YET IT WOULD NOT stop. Knowledge remained. *Don't put him in a metal box*—but they had, forever.

None of it made sense.

"We honor him," her parents said.

Even so, not to be in this house—not anywhere—not in the stable, the park, this whole world. Not here, this wrong universe.

It wasn't possible—she couldn't remember if the ugly long scar was on his right wrist or his left.

5. Malca, 1974, 1994

The whole year carrying the baby, there had still been the entryway, like an airlock on a spaceship, between the parallel worlds. Gavin was dead, but this child, *his*, was here, this universe. And then she bore her—Jeanne—and gave her up.

One afternoon, home from her first college year, Malca rolled tiny balls of red clay through her fingers. She lay watching the dogwoods on the gully's far bank. What life had been for him here. *I'm here, Gavin, I won't leave you.*

Except, it never helped. The damp smell of this clay could never open to the real world. Two years eight months now since the world died—and two years since she gave away the baby. It was as if these swaying leaves and shifts of light were minutes edging the universe like the bricks around a jail cell.

She scraped at the red clay, clawing the tactile wall aside, pulling stones out from the muddy bank as if to wrest away the wrongness of this futile end. Stones yellow, black, irregular. Until, just inches from where he had kept the blood-stained pack and tried to think his way out of those hours, trapped, were gathered, squeezed ino a narrow hole above a tiny ledge, a group of rounded little stones. There were twigs, too—short, some flattened.

Malca sat up; she twisted around to peer closer. Half the stones were light, half dark; half the sticks had brownish bark, the rest pale wood. Thirty-two pieces, in all, and two of each color had minutely carved manes. Chess pieces—an entire chess set. Had he left it because it was only for staying busy, for pretending there was reason? That phrase had been in his diary, "to pretend there is reason." Or something like that. The cops must have the diary. Unless they'd sent it to his papa. Why had his papa never helped him?

"There was some sort of service. His father wrote the court to go ahead with the burial." It was Dad who told her. "Bubbie, that does not matter. It's how he lived is what's important."

She remembered some of Gavin's songs, but not well.

Clutching the chess pieces, she pressed her nose against them, breathed in. The twigs rolled at the slightest movement, one nearly falling from her fingers. She mustn't lose them, must leave them here where he had made them, where he had lived.

Only, the wood would rot. Or someone could come by and scatter everything—a squirrel, a kid with a dog, even a horse like Dragon, pawing—though Dragon had been sold, according to the reply Gerilee finally sent, saying no one else there could manage him.

Reaching into her jacket pocket, Malca pulled out two fresh Kleenexes and carefully wrapped the pieces; she would take them home. So they would never be lost.

THE CHESS PIECES! FRANTICALLY, THE STILL-FLEXIBLE MATRON DUG through the geological layers of the storage closet. Both boys' preschool fingerpaintings and Jason's report cards with their A's and, on one, a teacher's scrawled "Highly assertive—please call," Marvy's still-fresh smiley-face *Kinder-Progress–1993* grade reports, a *New York Times* clip about one of Jeff's old cases ("exhilarating example of innovative immigration defense"), the "medievalists' view of Albigensians" piece she had written for *Smithsonian* back in graduate school, boxes of papers from her Sanctuary Movement days and the first two years of Human Housing Action, a wallet-size photo of a chestnut horse on very green grass, with "Dragon in Carolina" and "Hope you're fine, hon," scrawled on the back, the yellowing file folder with her court documents—she had forgotten those—attesting to "successful completion of two years' probation," Jeff's expired passport with its Czech and Polish visas from the European trip when they were first in love, the bluish-white tee-shirt she had worn the whole way down the Colorado mountain because on it lingered Gavin's scent, mixed up with hers—and the little white card with a pink and blue bunny, given by that hospital to every new mother, even those "relinquishing."

And there it was. The thin wooden box with the white tissue papers inside holding the twigs and stones, all packed away just as Mom kept, even now in 1994, in the old carved heartwood box, Granma's ancient photo of Chaim and her brothers—just as some Vietnamese parent must even today huddle, years past sobbing, over a slowly dissolving, long-crushed toy. Parodies of heirlooms.

Heirlooms. But the child was grown-up; she would have made contact by now if she cared, wouldn't she? If she was alive . . . No, she must be. The girl might want these some day.

6. Julie, 2001

So I told the group, "We take turns, I gather, at this show-and-tell?" But actually, I'm glad it exists, that there's an adoptee group around. And "Please," I said, "don't mind my snide remark; it's just an ex-Ivy habit—no, that's not intended snob. I didn't graduate there, anyhow. I finished at U.C."

And I told them, I'd needed an adoptee group for years; I really couldn't understand one bit why I'd waited. "But now," I said, "I've really talked to her, my birthmother. On the phone," I said. "I mean, it was her voice. I mean, her thoughts. I mean, *her*."

And I said, "Hey sure, I know you know, you who've had reunions. But listen, next week I *see* her. Here—she's lived here for years. Here. It's amazing, we each moved out to the Bay Area! Well, you can say 'serendipity' and possibly it's common, but . . . I mean, she's here. Hey, thank you, yes—I guess there's always lots of Kleenex for these meetings?"

And then I started in to tell it all. How Bill—he's not adopted, and I wish he were, he'd understand it better, all this crying . . . And the rest, just lots and lots of history.

How, of course, I always assumed I would find her. My "first mother," as my parents—they're ultra-lib—used to say. We were entirely agreed I should search. On this, they're wonderful. They told me they would even help me look, if I wanted—I don't remember when they promised that. When they said I was adopted? Maybe, but I don't remember—it just always *was*. The way the sun always set over the maple next to the garage, and the moon set over the Kahns' roof on the Fourth of July. The way the refrigerator lived by the kitchen door.

Philadelphia. I grew up in Philadelphia, until I was thirteen. Well, and other places. Then I came out to college at Berkeley, and stayed. Got to the Pacific and couldn't leave. Like everyone else.

Anyhow. When I was eight or so, some way I got the feeling—or before that, when I was five, maybe—I felt—I knew—that there was some strangeness, something scary or awful, in what happened. This wasn't very clear to me. I was darker-skinned than Ma or Daddy but that wasn't it; Tio and also Ariadne, two of my friends, were way darker. But something was wrong. I couldn't figure out what. I certainly thought it must be something strange with me, some reason I got given away.

Yeah, well—*all* of them had felt like that, all the people in this group. Incredible. But anyway, somewhere in there I understood that, whatever had happened, it was not 'cause of me. But it involved something dangerous—not something bad, but something to be avoided. And for a couple years, as it happened, I avoided it scrupulously. I was already ten or eleven before I even mentioned adoption again. But then Ma and Daddy explained to me that my birthdad had died unexpectedly. They said they didn't know how. She—my birthmother—had been "only a kid," Daddy said. He thought she'd been seventeen but Ma remembered the agency said sixteen. Hey, of course the precis sheet read "fifteen years of age."

Well, it also had "in the mountains," so usually I thought a skiing or maybe a horrible hunting accident. I avoided the thought, mostly, the next few years.

I was fifteen when they sat me down in the living room and told me—just a really primal sort of scene—"We know this much, and you're old enough to know now, too. You're a sensitive girl, but we feel you can handle it." That kind of thing. Then they said, "Your birthfather died violently," and that it had something to do with the police. They didn't say more, and I guess I was horrified, thinking maybe my genes were tainted and maybe—I would have to live with this, if so—maybe my birthdad had been a cop. So I didn't ask; what if they said yes?

But when I was close to graduation, and only a year from the Big Eighteen—I mean, when we're "old enough for information" and can search—they sat me down again. In the den—we were living in Annapolis, in Maryland, then, and had an old house with a paneled den, really a nice room. Anyhow, "He was shot by police," Daddy began, *letting it all hang out,* as he likes to say—they're ex-hippies, or try to think so. "Shot by police," he repeated, apparently not concerned about my chromosomes or reactions. Only, when I still kept quiet, he added, "Not drugs, Julie. They assured us it wasn't drugs."

But actually I was mostly wondering just what did happen—and whether it had, in some way useful to searching, made the news.

I know, that's not so uncommon a reaction.

Anyhow, that Wednesday I renewed my library card—doubtless surprising our branch librarian—and, downtown in the main stacks, I started going through old newspapers. I decided to do Washington D.C. first, since, while there are lots of mountains, there was just one city we knew they came from. I started looking at headlines for the nine months preceding May 12, 1972—that is, obviously, the nine months up to my birth. Looking for some sort of crime spree or shootout or something, where someone—I didn't know was it him or her—had a Jewish name. I didn't expect to find it.

But I did. Thanks to superb dedicated—and patient with me—librarians, and well-stocked archives and microfilm machines. Not just in Annapolis. Later, too, in San Jose and Berkeley, after I got out here, and once in Washington. Of course there were interruptions—lots of them, college and meeting Bill—well, and all of it—and, of course, having Gabriel. Having him and raising him, which seemed so terrifying—only partly for how weird it apparently made Ma and Daddy feel. So my searching took, with interruptions—mostly, interruptions—eleven years.

But it could have taken just a couple of months. Why? Because, perhaps weirdly, the "Hareen–Bernovski chase," as most the headlines called it, jumped out at me from one of the very first issues of the *Washington Post* that I saw on the very first day I researched. Needless to say, of course I ignored such a superstitious hunch.

You know, every time I researched, I'd come back to the newspapers. I would read any likely story but, over time, I saw that nearly none could possibly fit. It took years before I even remembered again that first old headline—but then I realized it might be the only story that could possibly be my parents'. So—this was about a year-and-a-half ago—one day I felt pretty sure (so many years after I should have been), or at least like I wasn't simply guessing. So I made Gabriel an early lunch, with the sugary Cheerios he loved that particular month. Then, as soon as I knew he would stay busy for a few minutes "reading" to his stuffed animals and feeding them Cheerios—though then later I would have to lift all the couch cushions, cleaning up crumbs—I went into the front hall and I picked up the phone. Of course, I could have waited for Gabey's naptime, but there's the three-hour time difference to D.C. They had a male receptionist and he sounded bored, but he connected me right away to a case worker.

Well, I spoke to her as if far more knowing than I was—expecting, I guess, that they would get very sporting, that the worker would say, doubtless chuckling, "Hey, you guessed it, that sure *is* your birthmom. Wow, we just can't keep these confidential records confidential anymore!" But of course instead I was, coolly though certainly kindly enough, given no information whatsoever. I was told they would send some "waiver forms." Of course, "only if you and your parents both sign"—that's how she put it—and only if my birthmother had happened to sign one too, would they ever disclose "your identifying information."

I just love that. Seems like protecting an organization efficiently is the most highly regarded virtue.

Well, so when I phoned again—it was only a week or so later—I pulled out my trump card. If in fact you'd call it that. Right after Gabey's birth, I'd had these pains in my knees—I thought at first, after all, maybe I had overdone my Fit-Mom workouts—and they got worse and lasted longer, and my legs finally became terribly weak. Well, when I went to the doctor, she was concerned, especially as there were these weird-feeling twitches, and she told me it looked like I might possibly have M.S. So, "For medical reasons," I told the agency, first by phone and later in a notarized statement, "information on the birthfamily is requisite. Due to hereditary factors."

Someone could say, I guess, "So why this bother? You had already figured it out." But we know better, we adoptees. We do want certainty—stability may be the word. I doubt others understand why we need that, why one feels, like Shakespeare's whatshername, so "storm-tossed." Lost above the abyss.

Like the people in a war who need to find some relative who's got displaced—misplaced?—but has survived.

Just who misplaced us, by the way—or rather, what misplaced us? What *did* all this?

7. Malca, 1982, 1989

Malca was nearly twenty-seven when she fell down the icy stairs outside Golden Hall. She was on the way home to her apartment after her "A" exams in the comp lit program, hands numb from writing, mind thick with the usually welcome immersion in abstract problems, contrasting Kant's moral imperative and Dostoevski's vision of ethical choice; comparing understandings of reality in *Phèdre, Hamlet, Germinal;* exploring relations among perception, knowledge, and action in *Beowulf,* Sholem Aleichem, and Tolkien. *Right,* she thought, as her foot—later, she was never sure which—slipped sideways, her patch-leather purse swung forward, and she landed on her back on the grassy slope beside the graystone steps. Overhead she saw thick elms, their wavy northern branches bare and cold. "Oh," she said. A man, a beautifully built, chisel-faced, dark-blond man, was staring down at her, pale skin around his sky-blue eyes crinkling in an incipient though sympathetic smile. But his lips were serious, his whole expression serious. "Then may I help you up?" he was saying in a deep voice, and she knew already this was very serious indeed.

They were together nonstop after that, heads close in conversation, hands laced across a café table, long thin arms and shoulders pressed together in unquenchable longing, cheeks and noses touching, as they walked the chill New England sidewalks through that evening and the next day and the next.

He was in law school then—Jeff Cohn, in his undergraduate years one of the top-ranking math majors in his class, oldest of three brothers and one sister in a family that had lived in New York State and Tennessee since 1866. A member of Harvard's swimming team, an Appalachian Trail through-hiker—"all the way from Georgia, Malca, and then of course you come down into the general store"—he was lively, strong, usually happy though "intellectually I'm naturally a pessimist," a lover of life who could track rare birds for hours, play peekaboo (during their second date) with a crying baby in a supermarket until the infant laughed. And he had strong ideals, ready to turn the legal system against social injustice, "if not quite to go beyond the law," even in 1982 when, as he put it, "What most these former rads want to remake is either their old potential or their new portfolio."

They had known each other exactly one week, taking long strolls through the Fine Arts Museum, holding hands and necking like schoolkids on the MTA, and sitting together, insecure enough to fear the other might really be studying, at the long library tables, when one night Jeff brought her back to his three-room apartment, tucked in a tower of an old Boston brownstone, and, unable to step apart, they collapsed on the dark plaid coverlet of his bed.

It had been so many years. Malca could feel the forgotten electric heat rush through her body. Not once had she responded to the groping students, not even to a pale young man she genuinely liked who had desperately loved her. *So many years,* she thought again, a half-hour later, her hands exploring Jeff's face, his warm skin tingling against her own as he moved to enter her . . . and suddenly she felt the empty mold-dark hopelessness of the bone-crowded grave that had opened with her womanhood.

"No," she cried—then turned her head, eyes averted from the beautiful man above her, despairing because this was the very cry that had turned away the two others she had previously thought to welcome into some first intimacy.

But Jeff did not run away—and did not merely hold her, as had her friend Jonathan, did not leave her to the graveyard loneliness. Instead, after several minutes' cuddling, wiping away her tears—and his own tears for this taut, bright young woman and "that poor martyred boy," and of need for her as well—golden-haired Jeff sought her body's depths again, and this time, entering fully, carried her up with him to his gleaming, bright-lit heights.

In the same way, because he never laughed, when she decried the pointlessness as wrong, "So just what sort of point could be enough?"— and because he neither waited out nor sought the telling, but simply heard her with what seemed real awareness of Gavin as a person, as an activist, a *man*—she finally told Jeff, as she had no one else, the whole story, not only "I loved this fugitive when I was very young, and he was killed, and I can't love anyone since," but the true account of who Gavin was and what they had been to each other, and the visions he had told her about life, and also of what had been lost, how he had died. The wrongness of it. The way the world had died, too. "Then I gave up our child." She ended there. She could say nothing more about the baby. She never mentioned finding the chess set; even now, she was not sure why.

She was twenty-eight, and she and Jeff could still hardly keep their hands off each other, when they married. "Your Jewish Aryan," Mom called Jeff, but obviously liked him. Mom was always teasing him, free with him and his siblings and nieces in a way Malca had never seen.

"He is *very* funny; he is an *honest* charmer," Mom explained, the second time Malca asked. Jeff and she were visiting her parents at the old Washington house. "Malki, that whole family—I don't know, they're German Jews but they're *haimische*—they're like home."

Dad said, "Well, Bubbie, I'm glad you finally have your life."

"When I get my doctorate, sure," she laughed, "a few credentials to change the world," trying to avoid the darkness, but Mom shook her head in warning—to which of them, Malca wasn't sure—and it did not seem worth arguing. She told her parents goodnight, then, and ran to where Jeff waited, tall and gleaming, her own white knight, in the darkened front hall, and they went out past the screendoor onto the lawn, listening to the crickets along the empty street in the damp thick pink-lit night of Washington, the remembered night.

"You do understand"—it could not have been the first time she had ever told him—"there is this other place in me. Because it will be there always, I think. Like a world where sometimes I am alone with someone else." Jeff had drawn her close, hand slightly twisting her long hair behind her head, and looked away, just like somebody stifling something; then he'd said, "Your poor courageous lover, I wish I'd known him," with such respect, and laughed so sadly, almost like her dad with her mom, that she gazed in admiration, stroking his chiseled, long-jawed face.

The next morning, while they were shoving their packs into the car to drive back up the coast, he had suddenly run his hand along her hair, all the way from the crown of her head down her back, and, adjusting the sideview mirror, said, "He *was* a good guy, wasn't he?" and, in the next breath, "Lord! I would have loved to take that case."

BUT ALREADY, A YEAR AFTER THEIR MARRIAGE, HANNAH, SHARPER THAN her premed profs had ever expected, and fascinated by psychology, was sounding the first warning. "Mister Understands-It-All, On-Top-of-It-All, Can-Handle-It-All," she said, watching with Malca from the dining table while Jeff chatted with their parents on the porch. "And what happens when you disagree with the particular point he's making?" After another year or so, at a picnic where Jeff noted that Mom's tuna salad had no plastic covering, Hannah whispered, "That man's Old Money, Malca—he's a winner. He sets his bounds, and you may take them or you may take them." Hannah still had to pack, that day, off on her fellowship to Leeds. "In England they understand there are neither losers nor"—she was playing with the silver filigree pendant that Granma had given her long before, running it between fine-boned fingers—"I dare say, Malca, winners."

Now Malca sighed, remembering, and looked around the sunny Berkeley bedroom; two of Jason's toy dinosaurs lay on the bed where the three-year-old had fallen asleep last night, and she listened to whatever species of owl was hanging out under the eaves. Well, as long as it was an owl, and not a bat. Bats were ubiquitous, here in the East Bay hills in summer, as Jeff had noted in one of his house-and-garden statements. There were more and more such statements lately, part of what she tried not to think of as his drift into household projects and his firm's "evolving future," and comments like "It's 1989, Mrs. Cohn-B. Times change." One day, maybe a month ago, he had asked, almost abstractly and out of the blue, "Your old boyfriend's conspiracy theory—it could have been true but isn't it a bit reactionary to still take that macho claptrap on faith?"

"Claptrap from people one loves?" she had snapped, then desperately tried to lighten the implications, laughing a bit, but had added, "So those cops just happened to take his stumbling for an attack?" She'd said no more, sorry to have shared even this. But surely Jeff could not be doubting the history but was simply trying to get her goat, irritated the way he so often was since they'd found she was pregnant again, or perhaps just picking at an old conundrum. But she wondered, putting little Jason's Legos away, if today Jeff still would "love to take such a case."

"Well, yes, your husband likes to say how great you are—until you seriously differ with him," a counselor had said. "Then we see just who it is inside those prince-clothes." It wasn't that Jeff refused to hear an argument, or even two; only, then he would begin his smiling—sweet but no longer taking what one said quite seriously.

Only, of course it must be more her own doing, their growing distance. Jeff did try—tried hard—yet there still were times she wasn't present, not with him in this world. It might not happen often anymore, but, she thought, stepping into the living room and putting the Telemann *Don Quichotte Suite* on the stereo, a truly whole person would be there fully for her family.

8. Julie, 1978

Cordotina. I was sure there was such an instrument, some musical device my parents and my teachers didn't know of—later, I thought perhaps some early-music instrument and I would go through the literature, trying to look it up. I was already getting my MFA when it finally hit me, I had simply mixed up two words. What Nicki played was a *concertina* but I must have thought of it as a *round accordion*, and somehow in my six-year-old, music-devouring mind it had become a *cordotina*, after which I just forgot the derivation.

Which does respond to your question—and hey that's what I like with this group, you may be sobbing, you may be laughing, but always you've got zitzy questions. And yes, there were times being an adopted child terrified me. Oh indeed, and the first I remember, and possibly the worst, was when the Witch said that only "borned people" could exist. Which must mean I didn't exist. The Witch was Nicki's mother, but that fact hadn't got through to me yet. Most of us—my friends Harriet, who was a year older, and Lucy, who was younger, and Jimmy, who was Harriet's younger brother—we would hide in the bushes in the alley, behind the Witch's house.

I'm embarrassed to think what we would yell at her. "Old hag witch, white-hair witch, we see you," and "Old Witchie, where's your broom?" Stuff like that; we were cruds. I mean, everyone would say we were charming, well-raised children, best of the middle class and that garbage. But the Witch was supposed to be mean, and besides we were sure, by her tight bun of hair and black squared-off jackets and raspy voice, she must be strict.

Anyhow, sometimes Nicki babysat me. She babysat the whole block. She was a rangy girl, fifteen or sixteen, very laughing, very friendly and supposedly a genius, and she had this cordotina she would play. Yes, the concertina. She liked certain songs, and so I came to like them too—Dylan songs and especially old Scottish and English ballads. One was the "Skye Boat Song"—the Prince Charles one, you know? She'd play me my favorites, too.

And I already loved music, really I did, so I wanted to learn this instrument, so Ma and Daddy said they'd pay Nicki to start teaching me, and one afternoon she showed up at our house and had me put my fingers on the keys—we had to adjust things a bit, since I couldn't reach them all—and I played, sort of. It was going to be a long haul, but I was thrilled.

But the next Saturday evening, when Ma and Daddy went out for Opera Night, Nicki was sick and so her mother came to sit with me instead. Yeah, the Witch.

Turned out, she was one. Very strict. So strict she said I had to go to bed at eight o'clock. And I couldn't have my evening juice unless I got in my pajamas first and brushed my teeth—by seven-thirty! Of course, I refused, and when she wouldn't let me get my juice from the refrigerator, I lay down on the floor and I started kicking—kicking her when she got close enough—and I screamed, "You witch! Witch, witch!" Until she got an arm through my defenses and jerked me up and shook me.

Well, that finished off the cordotina lessons. After my parents told Mrs. Nelson—yes, she had a name—that in our home we did not shake or threaten children, she must have ordered Nicki never to visit me again. I never did see Nicki after that, except from a distance. I hope she's done well. She gave me folk music, even some of the stuff I teach now. And how, growing up in that home, she became the young woman she was, I don't know.

But the thing is, while Mrs. Nelson was shaking me, she said I wasn't a "real child," I was a nastiness and I didn't really exist—"only borned children exist." For years I had nightmares about a witch. In some, the witch was my real mother.

Yes, and I became fascinated by epistemology, my sophomore year at Yale. The question, you know, of how we know that, for instance, we exist.

9. Malca, 1990

Malca was thirty-five, and nineteen years had passed since Gavin's death. Marvin was starting half-time daycare and Jason was now in kindergarten. Sometimes she thought that if she had only ignored Gavin's pleas, so young and panicked, that first afternoon, and galloped off to phone for help, or if later he would have given himself up and not fled the park, or, above all, had she just not, seeing those guns, groaned "Oh don't"—if only she had not groaned "Oh don't"—he would have long been out of jail by now, convicted of manslaughter at most. They had been too childish and scared. No, probably not—why, after all, had the police shot him down? "Brutally," a *Denver Post* reporter had written, but a Boulder paper had conjectured worse: "What truck bomb, indeed?" And, "Considering what we have learned since then of COINTELPRO," Jeff had remarked, back in the days before his doubts, "it's entirely possible they did intend it, love."

No matter—already Gavin had been dead nearly two decades. *Rotted and gone.* Not in a metal box, though. She had tried to find out, from the first moment when Aryeh, back in college, had explained there were ways. At the time, she could discover nothing; she wasn't quite twenty-one yet and, above all, wasn't "family." The only things anyone would tell her were public information. And these had come down to the location, which she already knew, of Gavin's grave.

The cemetery was thirty miles out on a neglected road, on a high slope that faced the front range of the Rockies. The first time she had gone, the snow had soaked her city boots and made them slippery. Tired from the flight, head aching, cold and damp, she could feel nothing. Until, like some cartoon character, she found herself down on the snow, lying across his grave, tears spilling so fast they made a puddle, snow melting around the edges.

But he wasn't there. It was beautiful in the white snow, but he couldn't see it.

She had gone back to the grave the next year, and again just before graduation—and every year until she married Jeff. *I will never forget you.* Through those years, it had been her promise.

Already, just before she graduated—it must have been during her last month in the college dorm—she had discovered a phone number in Cincinnati for Ahmed Hareen. It was he who finally told her about the coffin. She could never remember the first part of that call, except the man's "How did you find this number, Miss Bernovski? This is not listed. I do not answer." But he had recognized her name, and slowly the coldness melted. "I did make sure," he said at last. "A pine wood coffin, you see. They told me you kept repeating it, 'no metal box.' Besides, Miss, don't you think I knew? So be reassured." He sounded old and exhausted, someone empty in the way Gavin had always said of him, the way Mom and Granma had never been. There were long spaces of no words.

She shifted in the booth—a comfortable, huge booth into which someone, at some point in the dorm's history, must have stuffed the soft velveteen chair, too visible from the student lounge.

"I killed my son," the old man said.

She turned toward the wall so no one could see her face. "No. I know who killed him."

"Him, my wife, my family. Both families, first one and then one more."

She stared at her fingers, as if at the petals of a daisy. *I tell this man, I tell him not.* "No, this whole family, no. There's"—*I tell him*—"a child." *I tell him, sitting in this chair.* "You've a granddaughter. Our child. But I don't know where she is."

The old man had not answered. Only, stiffly and slowly, "Dear, I wish you well. I thank you for this call." And then hung up.

That must have been in 1979, maybe 1980. She must have been around the age at which Gavin had died.

But now, at thirty-five, she was one-half of a well-established couple, her husband not unwilling to explain that women's liberation had never meant a man could not just happen to be the more rational, and how ideals of relationships could turn into demands. Now, this hard autumn of 1990, she felt she was passing some prime of life, her own dad ill and weak, his heart giving problems so she always worried, always called Marvy and Jason to the phone, "Say hi-hi to Grandpa," thinking *What if this is the last time?* So much in the world was changed, Jason's little book on MLK showing the civil rights leader heading an anti-Vietnam-War march beside what looked like a French Resistance guerrilla, Jeff finding lack of *real commitment* if his dinner wasn't timely on the table, her last suede miniskirt finally given to Goodwill, and it seemed exceedingly unlikely that Old Mr. Hareen, as she thought of Gavin's "papa," could still be living.

Yet she had sent a so-called waiver form to the adoption agency, back in May, in case the girl came searching at eighteen; the Old Man should know.

No one answered, the first three times she called the Cincinnati number.

"Yeah, but it's not disconnected," Jeff said. "Let it ring longer." He acted amazingly disinterested; maybe he really was as "bored by all that" as he said.

A few days later, when she let the ring go on and on—it was two weeks before Christmas, the spruce outside the living room window hazy in the darkness, and she was in the middle of redoing fundraising letters for the mothers-and-babies project, and so anything seemed a good break—the weary voice finally answered the line.

Again it was hard. The man remembered her, he didn't object, exactly, and after a time he even started in about his guilt, but, for the rest, there were again mostly pauses, a silent resignation. She glanced through the bedroom doorway toward the kids' room, making sure Jay wasn't about to try any more "wrestling games" on Marvy. She couldn't tell how clear Old Man Hareen's mind might be. "You have a granddaughter," she reminded him.

"You already said this. Once." He paused. "I shall never forget."

"I'm certain she must be alive and well," she assured him.

"Never be sure, child."

Dear child. She shivered, remembering. The tears, the old ones, hung on her lashes, unexpected. "Do you know," she began, getting to the point, "about adopted children looking for their birthparents? If someday"—really, though, this was a dumb, futile possibility—"*if someday* she finds me, I don't have even a photo"—except two news clippings, but she would not think of them—"I've nothing from him."

"Nothing?"

"To show her." Only a carved bird, a chess set—and why was she holding back this fact?

There was the longest silence. "All right." Another pause. "All right." In that moment, she could remember how Gavin looked, standing beside the boulder and turning, eyes gleaming, repeating "No" and then "All right," changing his mind the way he did, looking across to where she waited by the firepit.

"I'll make you copies of everything," the old man said. "Photographs, all of it. I promise. And for the girl."

Through the door, she could see Jason pulling Marvy's Jumbo-Lego structure, block by block, down onto the rug. "May I"—she kept her voice polite, full of the modulated warmth learned in committee meetings—"instead come out to get them?"

There was no answer.

"Please. I want to meet you." She threw it out suddenly. "I want to see you." To meet this *Ahmed*, this *Papa* who'd never been there, after the first years, but whom he had loved. She waited, still watching for the moment Jay would push Marvy away, the usual moment the howling would begin. The Old Man might just hang up and flee again. "Mr. Hareen?"

"You want to see *me*?"

All she could think of was the young drawn face, the words "You held *me*?" She feared she thought somehow to see Gavin again, meeting his dad.

"Very well." There was a softer tone. "Come, then."

Making herself screen out for another moment Marvy's angry shriek and Jason's "So t'ere, t'ere, t'ere," she leaned against the wall. *Thank God. Thank God.* Only, she had no idea what this gratitude was for.

"Not yet."

She was swallowing her tears, still overwhelmed by gladness, when the words finally got through. "Not yet," the old voice was saying, over the receiver pressing her ear. "Soon. Soon—another year."

"Another year?"

"Or two—a few. Then you come. I'll call. I promise."

Each year, she waited but the call did not come.

10. Malca, 1995

It was not a logical necessity, after all, sibling rivalry. She and Hannah got along, now they were adults, even if Hannah's psychoanalyzing drove everyone batty and those questions like "Why live a continent away from Mom and Dad?" were awesomely guilt-inspiring. Anyway, Jay was gentle as a sheepdog toward Marvy, even though the younger boy, no little lamb, was nearly his brother's equal in height and also regarded by the grade school grapevine as "another Bernovski genius." Sure, geniuses—both were pulling on a barnacled rock, trying to turn it so they could, with great luck, catch some burrowing sand crabs. "Careful, don't cut your hands," she called, splashing toward them through the gentle surf. Very quiet today, long and rolling, the waves in the sparkling sun lower than usual for Stinson Beach. "Watch out, Jay."

But he didn't, and now the rock rolled onto his toe and he shrieked, tears flowing, and Jeff came running from the water, all dripping and salty, making a beeline for the medicine kit in the red pack, digging through the jumble on their blanket after it, waving it aloft and shouting as he ran, "Okay, okay now, Jason, got to avoid infection. Time for your alcohol swab, big man."

"Alcohol?" Jason stared up at the kit, the gleaming cotton in his father's grip. "Do I have to?"

"Well, no, would you rather swell up? You okay if your toes and foot turn lobster-red and you get sick? No—no, you don't have to." Jeff stood in front of him, waiting. "This doesn't work once it evaporates."

Marvy had come up, toes spread. Amazed, Malca saw him squeeze his big brother's hand. And Jay squeezed back. "It's okay, kid," Jay said, "I'm ready. Go ahead, Dad."

Our good kids. Her gaze and Jeff's met, silent. There were tuna sandwiches and cucumbers, celery sticks, apples, two kinds of cookies, more than enough even after the swimming. Everyone ate hungrily, and they were resting, nearly cool now, in the ocean breeze beneath the sunshade; the boys lounged in impossible postures in the middle of the sandy blanket. It was a red blanket, bought in the early days in Cambridge; she smiled, again catching Jeff's eyes; his hand reached to cover hers. She felt her skin yearn to that touch. Jay, toes now bandaged, held up his Hyperspace Wanderer comic book—he was "sidelined to the blanket" for the rest of the afternoon and trying to read all three comics before the ride home—and, behind the opened pages, he bent his head toward Marvy's and whispered.

"Yeah, they are." Marvy giggled, forgetting to whisper. "Their hands."

Jeff's long lips parted, elegantly lifting, pulling at her heart, her womb. The sun kept sparkling, out there on the waves. Seagulls walked the damp strand between the glinting water and the white warm beach. There were, in this world, sometimes such perfect days. She lifted his strong hand to her lips, kissed his palm. His eyes held hers like diamonds from the sky.

EXCEPT, THE WORLD WAS NOT QUITE PERFECT. JAY'S FOOT STILL PAINED him, and Marvy, tired, was picking fights the whole time while they trudged back toward the car. Jay hobbled, using a driftwood stick—someone's old broomhandle?—that Jeff had shaped into a crutch; Jeff himself kept yawning, eyelids red and heavy, looking even sleepier than the boys.

"I'll drive," she said, taking the keys.

"Thanks, m'love." He leaned over, gave her a kiss. A lengthy kiss. This time, they smiled before the boys could.

"Better seat them apart, love," Jeff said. "Wow, Marvin, you get to sit in back with me."

But of course Marvy wanted to ride up front. "Get your daddy strapped in, too," she called to him, turning slightly to check that everyone's seatbelt was cinched. Marvy was already nodding with sleepiness; beside him, Jeff was leaning back, eyes closed.

"I'm ready, Mom." Clearly, Jay had recognized the honor gained from using that phrase. Oh yes, genius, she thought, checking the gears before turning the key in the ignition. Hard to remember she once hadn't known how to drive. *If I had . . .* No, she mustn't go there now.

"OH MY GOD! OH WOW, LOOK. WAKE UP, GUYS—LOOK." SHE HAD pulled onto the unmarked turnout, here on the west flank of Mount Tamalpais. Already, the slopes of manzanita and California poppies shining in the sunset were below them; from this height, the first expansive views above the darkening waters had grown longer, wider; the distant blue Pacific shimmered glints of gold. Just beyond this vantage, the road wound upward through a stand of pines to plunge down past the forest east into metropolis, but here the world seemed a globe of silence, floating above the miniscule beach below and its adjacent cars, its stirring sleepy humans, its sandy rim drowned twice each day by tides.

"C'mon, guys, wake up."

"Hey, Malki." Jeff was stirring; she could hear his long legs uncrossing, sense him leaning forward, then felt his warm hand touch her neck. "Ah yes. Thank you." His lips nuzzled the back of her hair; she could smell the salt upon him, the sweet sea smells. "Thank you."

Jay was also sitting forward, too busy looking out the window to notice his parents' actions. She followed the boy's gaze.

Down below, beyond the paleness of the mountain slope, beyond the white line of the shifting surf, the green-blue sea swells hovered nearly motionless, the sun's last light reflected here and there upon the wide horizon-spanning surface. And from the pink-and-salmon sliver of the sky, four pelicans, gilded by the light, rose in a row and, one after the next, dove into the ocean, seeking fish to feed their young, and rose again, and dove, and rose.

"Wow," Jay was saying, and Jeff too, and then Marvy, wakened, echoed them—all her men sitting forward, heads as close as they could get to the windows, drawn by this wonder.

"Wow," Malca agreed.

And everyone kept repeating it, "Wow, that was incredible!" the whole two hours in the traffic jam along the freeway, heading toward the bridge and Berkeley. "Wow."

"Next time, let's bike it," Jay concluded, and Marvy said, "How many miles, Dad?"

"Well, let's count," said Jeff. "You first, honcho—wanta count?"

The count, he had called it, *but it's not a count. 'Cause we're each a universe.*

No, not to go there, not on this perfect day. Yet everything, he too, was part of it.

"I LIKED MOUNT TAM, MOM." MARVY REACHED UP FROM HIS BED to put his sunburned arms around her. She kissed him again, and then Jay—she herself half-asleep now. "My boys," she said.

"We're your kids, Mom." Marvy smiled, content.

And they grew up so fast. *All three of my kids.* "It's astounding," she said, climbing under the covers to curl against Jeff.

He didn't ask what she meant. He smoothed the sheet across them both. "Sunburn not hurting you, love?"

"Not yet. Kept out of it, mostly. Except in the water. You?"

"No problemo." His left hand arced along her shoulder, moved across her left breast, fingertip lightly stroking the nipple.

She gasped and turned to meet him. "Oh Jeff. Beloved."

If only he wouldn't try to silence so much, if only he hadn't silenced them both so many times, and if only she too hadn't given in too often, let things go. If only the road back wouldn't get too steep to seem worth the rough, long return. "Oh most beloved."

11. Julie, 2001

I still love that there are so many tissue boxes at these meetings. But here's the thing—not just that I'll be phoning her, "Malca," soon and all, but this. Two weeks ago, Ma sent me a newspaper, a Jewish newspaper. Even though she and Daddy never cracked a synagogue door since, I don't know, maybe thirty years.

Naturally, I got very curious.

Well, so I find this article, "Jewish birthmothers, Jewish adoptees." And I start trying to figure, and then I notice it takes half the page and the other half is ads for gourmet delis. And meanwhile my mind goes, asking why on earth would Ma send this? Until finally I see what the article's about. Loss. Are you surprised?

I was. So I asked, by email, "Hey, Ma, why did you send this stuff?" And she posted back, "I wanted you not to feel alone." She's a really good mother; I have good parents. I promise—right now—I won't hurt them.

12. Malca, 1996

Her first call from the hotel, he postponed the visit; the second time, he tried to.

"I can only stay three days," she answered, tired of the whole thing. She had waited patiently, she had kids at home, a husband. If Old Man Hareen wanted to keep running, let him—one of those "creatures so sensitive when they feel guilty they race off and people get really hurt," as Maggie in her women's group used to say. Maybe the old man's running had relieved his wife, but it had doomed his son. "We really need to meet today, if we're going to."

There was no answer. Just when she was about to hang up, he whispered his address.

The apartment was in one of the shabby-genteel downtown neighborhoods slowly re-gentrifying. A wooden staircase behind the brownstone led to the second-floor flat, its tiny porch overlooking a December-brown yard through a wide, bare maple.

"Come, come in." The small man, complexion pasty with age, was opening a screendoor cleaned until the metal netting shone. His old suit looked European, and the dark bookcases, the rugs on the living room floor, were elegant. So were the heavy-lidded black eyes and high cheekbones. Malca stepped inside, holding out the box of Italian cookies she had bought at the gourmet grocery in the terminal. "Mr. Hareen." She found she couldn't speak.

"Forgive me." It was a whisper, sudden and deep, his voice sharp-limned as the old frail bones. The man had apparently not noticed the gift. But he inclined his head, lips smiling. "Do not misunderstand, dear. I spend little time in guilt. Probably I should spend more."

Malca tried to smile back. Now he was thanking her for the cookies, one long hand touching the box. The resemblances were making her afraid, as if she would lose her remaining images of Gavin in these hollow cheeks or in the photographs inside the albums that—she half-consciously noticed—he must have brought out for her and stacked upon the coffee-table. It was a long table, placed before a couch, under the streetside windows. Ahmed Hareen's old eyes, much narrower than those she remembered, and lined with prominent blood-vessels, gazed back at her.

Those first months after Gavin had died, the crying had never stopped, nor in the months after relinquishing Jeanne. Years of tears—years of chewing her fist, as she was doing right here in this overstuffed living room, jamming her hand between her teeth to *stop this finally* and act like the middle-aged mother she was, calmly and politely meeting her host, this rather courtly, elderly man. Who would, she was sure, have been her father-in-law.

"It is all right." He was taking the box of cookies, so she needn't worry about spilling them, and he was guiding her, with a surprisingly strong grip on her elbow, to the red velour chair by the coffee-table. "Daughter, sit here."

THERE WERE SHEER CURTAINS ON THE WINDOWS, AND NOW AND THEN when her sobbing would break off, she looked out at the yellow and, later, darkening strip of sky over the rooftops. Traffic sounds and shouts pounded in from the busy intersection below. Old Mr. Hareen stood rigid for a time, then sat on a narrow desk-chair, body erect, the lines by his mouth deeply grooved, and watched her.

"HERE"—THE OLD MAN WAS HOLDING OUT A GLASS—"TAKE SOME wine. Wine is good, as your people have always said. And it will help, you know."

The room had turned nearly black. Neon light from a movie theater across the street glinted yellow—pink—yellow, changing each few seconds.

Is Marvy getting ready for bed? Probably not, probably Jeff is letting him and Jay stay up and watch the tube. While eating popcorn. No, skip that. Jeff was very capable, uncrushable; he'd know what to do.

"I came here a refugee," Mr. Hareen was saying. "My father, my first children, my wife were butchered in our war. When I met Gavie's mama, I cared again. You will not believe how we loved that boy." He put his own glass down. "Do not exonerate me."

The books on the shelves included two rows of very old, leather-bound volumes. Small and narrow, probably engraved inside. Granma had had tiny books like that. "Mr. Hareen, Gavin loved you. He said, 'Papa just feels guilty.' He understood."

There was a sound like a cough. The rim of the wineglass glittered against the wooden table. "You think that makes it easier?"

"His mom—he loved her too. He had her diary."

This time the sound was lower, a groan completely hollowed. "Did he tell you, Malca?" The old eyes were barely visible. "Did he say what happened—why she died so abruptly? I know—knew—my son; something made him slash himself."

Malca lifted her glass. She took a small drink, stalling. She could not—in honor to Gavin, in kindness to that suffering woman, in decency of any kind—tell this man everything. "Gavin said," she began, modulating into a head-office-staff tone, "that he knew the street scene. He said when they didn't give her enough medicine, he got her more. Quite a bit more." She tried to exude sincerity, looking into the helpless eyes. *Some things, you don't need to know.* "Gavin went out, one evening. He found her when he came home."

There was still silence. "After he slit his wrist," she began, confused, "I mean, when he was living in the park—" There were things she still couldn't speak of. "A couple days after they did that, I found him."

Mr. Hareen sat unmoving. She had to fill the silence. "He thought they were chasing him because he'd escaped that hospital. He thought they would 'shock' him. Shock treatments, he meant."

"Yes, he would have feared that."

She put her hand across her eyes. *You did nothing? And nothing while they hunted him down?*

No matter. Bones under the soil.

"You think I didn't care." The old man turned his glass around, put it back on the table. "We fight and lose them, and years come and we fight and lose. A time comes, we stop."

Hadn't Gavin told her? She had never understood what he'd meant, "It will always pull on me." He'd been so whole, so alive.

"Sometimes I would phone his mama—try to. She would hang up. One evening, no one answered, and soon they informed me. I flew to her funeral. Days later, I saw him in the ambulance." Mr. Hareen clicked his teeth. The long fingers with the slightly spayed nails were visible, pressing against the coffeetable in the recurrent pink and yellow light. "The boy was sensitive, a sensitive plant."

She looked away. "Don't I know."

For two or three hours, until the clock in the tiny kitchen down the hall read midnight and then 1 a.m., they barely said a word, the old man shifting, after the first hour, to one end of the couch, and Malca curled, unable to move, on the wide plush chair.

"May I turn on a lamp?" His voice broke the silence.

Embarrassed, she looked around the room.

"Refugees' children," Mr. Hareen said, as if to himself. "You're left to do our crying." Excusing himself, he went into the kitchen.

When he returned, he set out a tray of crackers and camembert and chèvre, with the cookies she'd brought and two tangerines and a bunch of grapes. "I am making a fresh pot of coffee," he said. "Do we go through the albums? Or you are too weary?"

She reached forward, shaking her head, and made herself take a cookie. By evening, she must be flying home—Jay would drive Jeff batty with his questions, "But *why* does A plus B equal C?" or whatever, piercing for attention like a cat climbing onto the keyboard. And Marvy must be worrying, "Where's Mommy, where?" Not to mention Jeff's dinners. But once she left here, Mr. Hareen would likely never again "find time."

He was opening the first album. "Tell me which you want. I shall make copies—I promise." As he spread the pages, something—love for this, his *second* lost family—trembled in his hands, bent his neck over forgotten scenes. She knew she must not ask about the diary—its excoriations, the desperation. She mustn't ask this old man if he had those pages—and the later ones full of the lost songs, stained with long-dried blood.

In front of her eyes was a sepia print of a turbaned man beside a very young woman hidden by a scarf and carrying two babies, while Mr. Hareen spoke of another time, and then, in black and white, a pretty woman smiled, incredibly straightbacked, graceful in a scoop-necked dress, and he was saying, with a gentle laugh, "That's Gavee's mama."

On the following page, the same elegant woman, head lowered, beamed into a blanketed bundle. "See, she's holding Gavee, there."

Malca jumped up. Quickly, she walked down the hall to the kitchen as if going for more coffee. The old man—his anguished expression was not meant to be shared.

Until dawn, they perused the pictures, "and, look, here is the constellation chart I made him," and old letters, and sometimes Mr. Hareen would tell of some event from what Gavin had called the time *before*. She kept asking for more stories, and the man kept speaking, and later, about 7:30 in the morning, she finally said what she knew he most wanted to know, that Gavin had recovered quickly and they had been happy (she left out the terror) in the mountains, and she told about the day Gavin put the neckscarf on her head and they'd laughed so hard, and how he would sing in the high cold evenings, and how he jumped to shield her, at the end.

"My mother," she added, "she still says—if someone mentions him, she says—'a mensch, he was a mensch.'"

Old Man Hareen walked stiffly to the window. It was after sunrise. "There was a drugstore out there," he said. "It had a phonebooth on a pillar out in front. The pillar was glass-tiled, blue, like a mirror. They used to park there and wait. There would be another car around the corner, usually a Ford sedan. Once, I think a week after it happened, I tried taking the train, not the train through Chicago, just a local, thinking I might transfer quickly. Still believing I could get to Washington and try to find him. You know, the minute after I got on, the one from that sedan came aboard and sat three rows away." He shrugged. "Also, the phone taps."

"So you couldn't have helped."

The old man turned from the window. "That's easy to say."

Malca straightened her back. "I wonder if it was all to cover up some accident—and smear the movement too, like he thought." But she wasn't wondering; the doubts that Jeff sometimes slashed across her mind were silenced here. She picked up one of the glass-and-amber stones, arranged like a crystalline shrub on the little shelf beside the chair. "Not that answers bring back anyone."

"No, none of them. I would like to meet my granddaughter someday."

In spite of the weariness making her want to never move, and the peace here that made her weak, Malca placed a hand across his thin wrinkled fingers, and she said, "I am so glad." For that instant, her heart leaped. But her eyes saw only those other long fingers, mud-stained as they pressed a tiny stone beside the creek, and—because even this long-hoped-for sharing of the sadness could not change what was—the hole in time without an end.

13. Julie, 2001, 1987

What people don't get is the ethnic bit, even now. I mean, I'm Jewish, as most people know from my name, but awfully dark Jewish. And don't think there's no more racism.

When we moved to Annapolis—it was the summer after I started high school—the heat was even worse than Philadelphia. I loved being in a smaller city, the Chesapeake Bay and the fishing boats nearby, and having beaches so close, but the climate . . .

It was not so much the weather climate, however. My big problem, not really with my schoolmates but some of the new neighborhood kids, and to a surprising degree with older people, especially storekeepers, was that Annapolis is Maryland is the South. Some people would see my dark skin and not even talk to me. Even in Ma and Daddy's Jewish circles—not religious, of course, but Jewish—where you would expect to know better, some people sort of smiled and fanned their space. Even kids my age.

One time, I was at a "junior social" where we were supposed to learn "ease with the opposite sex"—a joke, considering some of my friends were practically living with their boyfriends—down in old-town Annapolis. A narrow, echoing rowhouse, it was, and you could hear very well around corners. So this one girl I barely knew, pretty, named Annette, who dressed like a Sixties hippie dressing up as a slut—that's the best I can describe it—was saying to another girl, I forget her name, "Oh, half-Jewish, they say, so let's just hope the Jewish half was Sephardic. Otherwise, I dunno, could be they adopted a Darkie."

I mean, twenty-plus years after the Civil Rights Movement, "a Darkie"!

Actually, there were some Blacks around—no one in my school, you can imagine, but the woman who came in the day before Passover to help Ma with spring cleaning, and the guys who ran the "Crabs 'n U" store. And once in a while somebody, maybe at the recycle, would call me—you ready for this?—"Miss Julie." For real.

Yeah, to them I was Whitey, "olive" or otherwise. Guess I can't win. But, in all seriousness, Ma and Daddy couldn't take that climate, either. A year after I started Yale, they moved up to New York State, to Albany. I got farther away, of course. Though I could not really say why I left Yale for Berkeley—certainly wasn't the music department. And I don't believe that stuff—that subconsciously I knew I'd find my birthmom out here, or like that. Obviously.

14. Malca, 1998

What Malca was most grateful for was that Mr. Hareen's stories had confirmed her knowledge of who Gavin was and what he'd told her of his past, strengthening the battered certainties that—even now in this stockmarket-obsessed summer of 1998—she could hold onto.

Malca looked around Marvin's room, the Startrek cards taped over the bed where he lay snoring, his chrome-cluttered bike shoved into a corner since he feared someone could steal it from the garage.

But the truths of these childhoods and this home were never enough.

The past few months, the way had felt cluttered. Time seemed collapsed, its layers lost in sameness without seasons, and confused. *I'm aging and my memory is slipping.* No, that wasn't it; she wasn't standing up enough to Jeff's arguments, was all—and not only his, but the whole drift in worldview.

"Puritan cynicism, isn't it?" she had confronted him, one rainy evening three months ago. "We're all guilty? Just dig harder and you'll find it"? He had scratched his cheek, peering into the dresser mirror, and said, "If I may remind you, love, you don't actually know Gavin didn't do it. You only had his word." Vaguely she'd remembered Jeff saying this before—and herself shrugging it off, since sometimes he tended to pick arguments to keep away whatever he didn't want to discuss. Never had she told him her certainty, on the long trip down the mountain, that the redhaired FBI lieutenant on the small white horse had kept back a secret from those Colorado deputies—the secret of Gavin's innocence. But of course, after those nights in jail, she had never felt entirely sure she'd really seen the FBI man unfurl the headline to the sheriff's gaze, "'Truck bomb, what truck bomb?'" Nor had she told Jeff of "the count"—what Gavin must have meant by that, the innocence of his vision. And she hadn't said a word of what Old Man Hareen, after their meeting, had phoned to add, "That corner—it was not Flag Day when police began to stay there, but earlier. Four days earlier—I saw them first the evening I picked up my summer jacket, thinking how late I'd let that go. You understand, they must already have had plans."

But on that rainy spring evening, after Jeff, scratching his cheek, repeated his accusation, he had showered, sweaty from taking the boys "to sharpen up their basketball game—won't hurt them," and put on his favorite workshirt, skipping dinner since they'd shared five-and-a-half hotdogs at the game. Stretching out on the bed, he watched her read. "What are you thinking?" she asked, puzzled.

"Actually, about your ghost. Hey, at least it's distraction from basketball." He sounded exhausted, so why would he bring this up now? "Keep in mind how much we never know. You can't be sure why he died."

"They shot him. To prevent a trial." It seemed too wrong, though, her and Jeff speaking of Gavin as if chatting—and chatter, besides, that could accidentally open the old wound. There must be some reason Jeff had brought it up, something today that he wanted to avoid—or to launch at her—and she clutched herself, arms tight around her chest.

"You think." For a moment Jeff breathed more slowly. He lay there with that athlete's calm, in trained stillness, and she feared what he might say—surely something about their differences. And so, at first, his words were a relief. "You know"—he turned toward her, leaning sideways on an elbow and again scratching his weathering cheek—"we both know, really. Look, time gives perspective, after all. Would it be so terrible if the fellow actually did bomb it?"

No—no, it wouldn't. Because maybe more people would be alive now if we'd all done that. But she didn't want to go that route; at some point she had understood what Gavin must have known. And what he'd known, the horror he had recognized, was just what Jeff meant by *If the fellow actually did it.* Her lip curled; she could feel the motion. "You're joking, yes?"

Jeff's blue eyes stared, serious enough. "Hey, everyone was for blasting out the war machine."

"That's not how I remember it."

"Touché." He stretched his legs. "Still, you know he could have tacked on the suicide stuff, all that, whatever. We can't ever be sure."

I knew him. It was the only argument she'd given herself, even among the mountain pines on the night when Gavin told her what he'd really done.

But that history was too private—she made no reply.

And this was too bad, because probably her silence at Jeff's accusation, while they listened to the thick spring rain, was what had, through these past three months, let a tiny doubt work in. But if she'd argued the point with Jeff, it might be worse. Because he never would really engage it; he would hear her for one sentence—one round—or maybe even two, then let her go beat her mind against a shrug, a dangling bait of silence; it was one of his ways to *win.*

Jeff did not bring up the subject again, of course. It was among the many points they avoided. Always it had been this way—the gentle, almost courtly understanding and then, if she challenged him too long, the nod, the soft "I see," and a yawn or silence. But more and more the issues skirted close to principles. His firm, Levitt and Cohn, was slowly moving from immigration and civil rights into general litigation, though he still remained its immigration specialist, occasionally moonlighting as consultant to Latin refugee advocates. "I continue this work, to the extent practicable," he would tell their friends, usually at some dinner party, "but Malca and I, we have a significant mortgage. Not to mention the pediatrician. What brings down the most barricades, as we bring down the '90s, is the college-fund account."

Everyone would laugh, she too—even when he added "Not that you would know this, given Malca's love for a nonprofit pittance"—because, whatever their problems, she and Jeff belonged to each other. Indeed, she felt full, these years. Her body still glowed its love for her husband, as his for her, yearning magnetically toward each other across the busiest party, the coolest memorial for victims of Hiroshima or the Holocaust or Vietnam, the hippest Housing Action fundraiser. Jeff's wit and elegance would burst upon her, like the amazing fact of his desire for her, at moments like joy itself, and always there was the serene, exhausting, welcome happiness of the boys.

But if she too laughed, agreeing with her husband and the others that "We're way too decrepit for those barricades," and knowing the changing gestalt was hardly his fault and besides he still put in plenty of pro bono hours, part of her stood off in anger, thinking *I work sixty-hour weeks so people have shelter, I go to rallies, I hang posters, phone officials—I will never join this despair-of-convenience*, and all the rest that she meant but had no way to make them see. She would not give up what once had been. What Gavin and she had known.

The night after their dinner party, back in April, she had put the silver engraved earrings back in her jewelry box and pulled from its narrow drawer the folded celestial chart that Mr. Hareen, saying "Gavie always brought this to the lake," had handed her. Smiling, opening the blue-black printed paper, she had stared at the faded stars.

Now she gazed at the glow-star stickers Marvy kept arranged in constellation patterns over his bed. He and Jason were down in the garage with Jeff, fixing whatever on their bikes. They were learning quickly, Jay doing nearly all his own repairs now. "If your parents or somebody hadn't been so old-fashioned, you could do this yourself," Jeff had told her—how long ago?—when they were dating and she had asked for help unclogging the bathtub in her old apartment. His words then had made her feel alone; now she was alone again.

"Not like your single golden summer of fond youth," some woman had said—the therapist Ruth? Or someone down at Human Housing, the evening they all went out for drinks and got blotto?

Malca sighed. Automatically, her hand smoothed a wrinkle on the chintz cushion of the rocking chair. Marvy still liked that chair; she and Jeff had loved it.

We used to have treasures together. This was nostalgia, as if time's knots weren't tangled. This was the nostalgia that Jeff thought he saw when she dreamed of Gavin. Nostalgia—remembering the years of her-and-Jeff as something already ended.

Only, it must not be ended—for the boys' sake. For Jeff's.

And mine. She stroked the pinecone pattern of the chintz, pleased.

Would it have mattered, what she and Gavin might have found and loved for their home?

15. Malca, 2000

"Not just a new century, a new millennium! Today nobody naively counts ballots, Vietnam is a vacation destination just like Auschwitz, half the population thinks books come from Oprah—but for you, Malcae m'love, relationships are still Victorian romance." Out the window, people were standing on porches along the curving hillside street, shooting fireworks and toasting the year 2000, "Y2K," with merlot or champagne. Someone on the road below was celebrating with pistol shots. On the television, a ball fell, as every hour on the hour all around the globe, heralding New Year in Times Square.

"New York moment, that," Malca said. She tried to ignore Jeff's dig.

A full minute earlier (*back in the old year, in the second millenium, the old days, ancient history*), he had cautioned, "Truth is not always an affordable luxury," in remonstrance to her tears.

She hadn't intended those tears. *I know you love me. I know you're not about to walk on outta here. But—*

He had not answered her question, only responded, "You know very well, dear, you come first in my heart and my soul. Because, if by now you cannot see that, perhaps really we ought to—" and *Oh lord, another of his ultimatums*, she had thought. But by then he was letting it go, changing the subject. And that was all he would explain, back in that moment in that century—no, millenium—about his trip, "next week sometime" up to Lake Tahoe, "alone, love. I'm meeting with someone."

She did not sip from her drink. "Why tell me this tonight, Jeff? Because 'everyone is miserable on New Year's'?" Her voice shook—but, after all, she was sick of his stonewalling, of having always to struggle to stay whole against his long defining of their world, of worrying whether this time he really would be meeting *someone else.* No, if Jeff ever left her, maybe it wouldn't be the end of everything, not at all.

"Why tonight?" she repeated. *Just say it, Jeff, please. Say, "So you will feel alone—to let you know how I feel."*

But he didn't.

Leaning in the front doorway, lifting her wine cup as their neighbors—professors and a doctor and at least two social workers, some with teenagers like their own—lifted glasses, up and down the block, and watched the New Year enter the East Bay on the unseasonably warm cloudy night, she finally took a sip. She heard her husband's careful breathing. He knew how to handle things, always had. He didn't say a word.

THAT NEW YEAR, TOO, TURNED TO MORNING, MONTHS WENT BY, and Jeff never spoke of the outing again, either before he left or after he returned; nothing changed, except that the long-congealed silence of things only thickened.

16. Malca, 2000

This new loss. And only two months into these changed dates, with their strange initial numerals 2 and 0.

"Malki, your dad always defended me around his parents." Mom was wiping at tears now as if they were part of life. Sobbing between sentences and making little hiccoughs, turning to look back toward the yahrzeit candle on the fake-wood mantle.

"Easier for Dad's heart, we thought, an apartment." Mom had explained it again, perhaps an hour ago. Malca stretched her arms out, running a hand along the torn place in her garment ripped for shiva. "He knew," Mom was saying, "they'd stop refusing once we married. That's why they sent us those lamps—to mitigate themselves with cast-offs from their piece of Tennessee. French originals, nineteenth century. Nothing I would curate, though." Mom waved a hand, probably even now missing the solid feel of a cigarette. She was studiously not looking at the lamps, their Empire pastorales hand-painted on thin porcelain. "They would twit my accent, Malki. I was 'your babushka' when they thought I didn't hear. This never changed. But he stood up for me, always."

"I know." She remembered, long ago, Mom crying "They laugh at my accent," and Dad and Aunt Ellen slightly smiling across a dining-room table, blood-red walls behind them.

"A mensch, your father. Like your first husband." Mom must be forgetting, or maybe not caring, that Jeff sat just beyond the doorway in the living room, speaking with their guests. "Because who was I? Not some Southern Jewish belle in shiksa clothes, not some well-educated graduate student, but a refugee. A scrapheap person, like your Human House picks off the streets, a little fileclerk, 'Is it *q* and then *r*, Meestar Berknowski?' But your dad saw. 'Here,' he told me, 'let's do the research.'

He taught me the subtlety of English, the literature. One month afterward, in the Library of Congress, we kissed. He kissed me."

Malca shifted. The straight black chair was right for this sorrow; discomfort should not matter. If, in fact, any of it mattered.

Out in the dining room, Hannah's voice rose, nearly shrieking. Jeff answered quietly, "See, that proves it," gaining a point, and Hannah replied, gone quiet too, "Some people never learn to compromise."

Right. But it made no difference. Malca stared down at the carpet. "How old were you, Mom?" One had to say something.

"Nineteen. It was 1952. We had to—"

"Then you hadn't been here long."

"We come as strangers." Mom's words fell from a pasted smile, taking on the fractured English of a refugee trapped in Manhattan until heading south with Granma to find something better than shelter kitchens and an airless room.

"And in D.C. we try one synagogue, we try the next. They say, 'Go, go.' But this time I say *No.* I say, 'We are here, here we stay.' One woman—" Mom's eyes swiveled toward the yahrzeit candle. Her mouth compressed.

"It's all right." Malca squeezed her wrist. *She used to tell us stories, Hannah and me.*

"One woman, she gave us a bed in her remade garage, a place to stay. This is why." Mom smiled. "This is why your dad and I reach our hands during seder reading, every Passover, where we say, *For we too have been strangers in the land of Egypt.* Why we always touch, always. Did touch, I mean."

Now it was Mom needed help. In this time. *I used to think you were used up; I felt so guilty.* Long ago, when she had told Gavin about Mom, he'd listened, probably.

"Understand, your dad and I never tired about each other."

17. Julie, 2001

"Thanks for this excellent green tea," I told them. "I'd come to meetings for the snacks." And I yacked on and on, more tears and more, like everyone else in this group. "You'd think," I said, "we'd have teared ourselves out. Or is it the election? Sobbing in advance, figuring how they'll clomp us down? 'Back to anonymous records, you little bastards.' Also, doubtless we'll have more racism. And, believe me, skin like mine, you get very aware of it. No, you're right, not around here, but just try taking a vacation."

Well, then the others made me get back to the point. So I said, "Hey look, I was crying all yesterday, and two days before that. Just constant—cry, cry, cry. So there I was," I added, "sitting right there on our kitchen floor—I'm practically drooling, I'm nearly crawling across the floor, not even looking over at my son who's kicking in his highchair to get down. And there's me, you can imagine me, crying away and my "Impeach before Gotterdammerung" tee-shirt by this time all drooly, and trying not to pee. Right—so now I laugh, I make a joke, and here we are, the lady's sobbing away again. Doesn't seem real.

"It doesn't—I'll be seeing *her,* real soon."

18. Malca, 2001

The seagull still circled, seeking a way back home, but Malca, phone in hand in the tiny office looking toward the Golden Gate, barely saw it. Through the wallboard, some young guy in the next room made a whoop, a high sound like a siren, "Your *supervisor* said so? *Said* so?" and the Kleenex in her hand had got too wet, the first already soggy, so she wiped the sleeve of her blouse, a blend of silk and cotton threads, across her eyes. The sky was pale now and the gull slipped suddenly around a skyscraper and vanished toward the sea.

"I've had good parents and a happy life so far." The young voice across the line was choking up so Malca wanted to hold her and heard *I'm alive, I am here.*

"Where are you?" Malca's own voice was strangely deepened.

"Here. I mean, San Francisco. Bill and I, we have a condo, it's all we could afford—we should be glad even for this."

"I know. We're in Berkeley, it's crazy here too." All the usual stuff, rolling on, sounding just like an ordinary conversation—the expenses of the city, the young husband's underemployment, Jeff's caseload, how the market slump was hitting Human Housing Action, Julie's hopes to "get back into fulltime, soon as Gabriel's older." The child—no, not a child, this woman was twenty-nine—paused. "Your grandson, Gabriel—see, he just turned three last week."

"Gabriel." The rainbows had come back out of the other world.

"We want more kids, but not yet. Hey, Gabey's very bright, very. Very active." *Very our family.* The young mother laughed.

"I would have kept you, Julie."

"I know—I know that. I was 'Jeanne.'"

"You know?"

"It all must have been too awful." The young voice broke. "I read those newspapers."

"We need," Malca managed, after a minute, to speak. "We need to meet. If you wish?" Everything hung in the question.

Sharp arguments still splattered through the pasteboard wall and another gull (or was it the same?) circled the bubble of sky.

LATER, MALCA REALIZED THE GIRL HAD SAID "OH YES!" AND THEY HAD somehow managed to work out details. They would meet the next week, the next Friday, "Just us, Julie, this is our first moment, practically. The nutty holiday'll be finished and we can concentrate, and you'll be past that awful interview. Let's say noon, okay? Maybe noon on the twenty-eighth?" In a park in the Berkeley hills, Julie suggested, "Maybe under the merry-go-round overhang, in case there's rain?" Malca laughed. "And if you're late, don't worry, it's all right. We"—she heard the girl laugh too, in the joy of it, the new communion, the sameness of their humor—"can probably wait just a few minutes more."

19. Julie, 2001

"**B**ill, my birthmother loves me—loves me."

I wanted to go shout it from our rooftop, or at least from our magnitude-6.8-proof little balcony, and hey I think Bill knew. The moment before I spoke, he was all over my body, out here in the kitchen, his workclothes off and his hair washed, damp from the shower, smelling divinely but groping like a rutting animal; then, as soon as my words came through, "I am happy for you, Jewel," he said, and took my hand almost bashfully, and I knew he understood.

An hour later, though, he was into the strong macho beastie again. "This silence stuff's a real turn-off," I said—dumb move, actually.

Even his ears went pale.

"Oh Christ, I didn't mean it that way." Lot of good that did. Wow, was I being cranky. But it was hard, putting up with anything, anything at all. Because of what *finding* is like. Finding is like being swallowed. By paradise, by terror. "I didn't mean—" I gave it up. "You do understand, I know you do. My birthmom loves me."

His hand was still damp against my breasts. "Duh, Ma'am, so do I."

I squeezed that hand.

"Hey, Jewel—?" His voice went so low and hesitant it was scary. "How do you know the woman isn't after something?"

I guess I figured, *Hey, wow, skip this.* Or I might have said something really, really awful—unforgivable. At the least there'd have been one major argument. So I made my voice go soft and furry. "Bill, it's all right, sweetheart. Hey, dear, come here, come to me. Come, love." And so on, and so on—and slid myself down until I lay right underneath him, right here on this clean, hard, slippery floor.

So pretty soon there we were, going at it nude as Eden, and the crying begins. Mine, I mean. Not from frustration, either, just tenderness—for Bill who loves me, and for Gabey sleeping in his crib, and also for this woman who once loved a man and then gave birth to me. She was a mother, like me.

That was when—right then, my body going up and down beneath Bill's thrusting, and both of us starting to throb with our very *very* mutual heat—I decided hey, I'm not gonna tell my birthmother I've got M.S. Let her think I am unflawed as any newborn, pure, untroubled, and pristine.

So, not much later, there we are lying around, me on Bill's lap, right in front of the yacketing television, him stroking my forehead, and that long lank of his own hair curling down across his eyes so he really looked cool, and "Julie," he says, "Jewel. My jewel."

So I says, "Wow, I'm scared" and try to explain—like a cave and I am falling in. And all he does is repeat "Jewel, my jewel." Yet I think he really knows what I mean, what all my crying means—*My Mamma loves me. Mamma, why did you throw me away?*

And his big hands keep patting me, silently seeking to overcome this helplessness the same as when I first got diagnosed. In crises, Bill shows his devotion. I didn't have to explain my crying, either. Which was like those sobbing fits—wow, I'd forgotten those—when I was a kid. My parents would come into my room then, stepping around Lovey, the rocking horse, and then, looking sort of ill and as if they knew far more than I, they'd say, "You miss your other mommy. We know she would have kept you if she could."

Of course, they knew nothing of the kind.

Bill kisses me, just as if I were a little baby. As if he knows what I am feeling, *Don't leave me this time, Mamma.* Like all the losses of the world.

I am falling into chronicity. I need a foundation, some means to absorb this universe.

20. Malca, 2001

But this time it was real, Gavin kneeling there, his skinny fingers barely touching her eyelids, so light she smiled at this fragility, and indeed it was impossible his lips were pressing upon hers, but they were. Those seeming-memories of his death, of life gone on into a hardened world, were only nightmare; he was here. Lifting toward him, slipping through this forest, laughing, *Gavin Gavin!*

She felt the new pain smash her fingertips against the waxed wood of the nightstand.

"God, no."

Fog, thick late-December fog, cloaked the spruce and distant hills beyond the window; a trace of predawn turned the room—this room, in this world—almost lilac, like a bruise.

"I am so sorry." She saw the thin lines of age, the slightly cleft chin, of her husband's face. This was the fourth time the world had opened since her daughter's call. "Please hang in."

His eyes didn't even look sleepy; he must have been long awake. "For what, Malcae? For you to finally take notice that your teenage years are over? That it'll be our turn all too soon?"

Snow had layered on the stiff green bag, weighted the body trapped inside. "Once I've met our—met my daughter, then . . . This Friday, you know?"

"I'm a person, too."

She reminded herself she must listen. After all, this too was happening—here, in this grey and blue world where one of Jeff's high-arched feet stretched out from under the ivory blanket and his warmth lay close beside her, his hiker's beauty that even now could make her choke with happiness. Or could whenever she forgot there once had been a different happiness.

"Give me these hours, Jeff. A couple more days." *I do love you, but leave me alone.*

"But suppose it's not just hours? Dear one—dearest one—I'm not so 'secure' as you think. Your dad with your mom, ghost-keeper and all that, I'm not. Not to mention, your mom went through worse, lots worse, without this sort of crap." His breathing was getting fast now—working himself up. She ran her fingers over his forehead but he wasn't stopping. "What's it even about, Malcae? Do you actually know who that boy was?" Abruptly, he sat up. He grabbed her hands and pressed them down against the bedclothes. "Try therapy or something, can't you? E-M-D-R."

"Forget him, you mean."

"I thought you loved me."

That stiff look over his mouth—holding back again. *So here we go, Jeff.* "You'd rather think I don't?"

No answer.

Tonight she'd make chicken croquettes for dinner, a favorite of his that she never took time for. But he must be very frightened. No, angry. No—no, he was leaving her.

Only, his strong arms reached around her waist to pull her toward him. "Malcae, Malcae." The deep throaty voice spoke in her ear, the voice that used to win so many immigrants a stay of deportation; its tones encircled her. His long hands stroked her thighs, lips pressed her throat. She leaned into his strength, this man whose vital grace was her other home.

You knew the guy five months, for godsake—he had said it again last night. Yet even this was better than when, those years the boys were small and his disillusionment had not yet shifted into politics, he would go cold and stiff-lipped if she dared mention Gavin at all. And really their flare-ups were so few, their bad times shouldn't even count. But, though at first Jeff used to say "I'm glad you're a person who won't forget someone she's loved," now he wasn't saying anything, only working on her like a slick machine. His hand stroked far too hard, his tight smile turned insistent, rough; his body plunged, abruptly and too swiftly in harsh sharp long thrusts. He was—she understood—lost, furious, frantic.

And the problem was, she couldn't care. "Soon—in Tilden Park on Friday. I'll see her, Jeff, I'll see my daughter." Words to distract him, yet to try to bring him back—to pull the worlds together in one universe, at last reopening.

"But don't you understand?" He lay still, breathing hard, beside her. "If I were so secure with you still loving that boy, don't you see, what would that say about my love for you? I give my whole self—can't I expect you to give yours?" His fear, then, so long held down beneath the hundred definitions. She patted his hand, breathing in rhythm but quietly, trying to quiet him, feeling his love and desperation.

"However, Malcae, since you won't—"

Only, none of it seemed separate from the stillness, this early dawn grayness where she floated between-times, waiting.

Downstairs the boys had already clicked on the television, frightened as they'd been all week by the approaching advent of that previously legendary Older Sister, and the news came floating up, accounts of yesterday's bombings of Afghanistan, spoken in those constant tones of righteousness; since the attack back in September, such furies of revenge stalked everywhere, hunting for some adequate "perpetrator" as they once had hunted Gavin. Seeking somewhere, anywhere.

"Dear one." Jeff's hand was on her arm. "Don't go there. Please."

She turned, fingers seeking his tousled hair. To lean into him, secure in his certainties, these known walls. "My daughter's coming"—what a tired explanation.

His lips curved, the skeptic's smile. "You are not thinking 'daughter,' you are thinking ghost." His hands moved through the air around her head as in a courtroom battle, struggling to evoke whatever he must. "And understand, I am not angry and you are not frightening me, love. But do you even know what's going on around you? Have you seen Marv's terror, and Jason's? Do you—sometimes I wonder—even comprehend what's happening politically, what's been lost this fall? No, you don't. Because you *can't*. Because you are not free to see new loss, not separate from your own." His hands clamped her wrists, too firm.

Let go, let me be. She lowered her head.

He wasn't letting go, though. His words came out staccato, pained. "Therefore—and, as I was about to tell you—since you cannot choose, you soon shall find you *must*. Either your ghost, or else to simply mourn him. Either chimaera or reality. Either death or life." The pressure of his fingers tightened, though his upper lip lifted as if to show he laughed at his own rhetoric.

Doublethink games. Besides, what made him think there was a choice? But she didn't fight his grip.

"A simple either-or, dear one. Not both—metaphorically speaking."

Choose life. A thousand times, she'd heard those words. *Blessings.* On the sloping granite, Gavin and she had chosen life.

"However"—Jeff's hands were lock-tight—"there is one other choice. And, believe me, I never thought I'd say this. But there it is, and it's a choice you will soon have to make, love. Because otherwise you are edging into another sort of loss." His voice sank. "Well, you know, Malcae, 'me or him.' 'Him or me.'"

Those elegant lips, sardonic now. She opened her mouth—to kiss them, to speak.

"He or I," Jeff repeated.

Then she did lean forward, and the silence of her kisses touched the curling lips, and slowly began to move down. Carefully they sought his silk-haired chest, his youthfully taut waist, and soon, as her knees bent, they caressed the insides of his muscular thighs. *Jeff, have you ever followed your ultimatums? No. No, you won't leave me.*

Unless, of course, he would. But wasn't that the point, to keep her guessing?

Around them, the room looked dingy, stale. A new paint job was necessary but they had decided they could not afford it. Jeff's hands let go her wrists, moved gently now upon her abdomen. "Let's take the boys," he said, "to that holiday vigil tonight." Meaning the peace vigil at U.C.—after he'd avoided practically every demonstration of the past ten years. Grabbing this tiny shred of truce, she looked up, nodding. He said, "Those bastards in D.C. You'd think, after seeing those people in those towers die, they'd come up with something better than more bombs. Sorry, love, that's hardly news."

He rubbed a knuckle. Then he laughed and with both arms pulled her down onto the wrinkled sheets. "Oh God, we need ya, love."

She peered through tears into his face. His long lips pressed together; she sought their elegance, a meaning. "We need ya here," he repeated, "not way out there in space."

I need you too, Jeff.

His hands moved, silk now. "Not off somewhere with that kid who conned you, that killer like the rest."

Past the window, beyond the plum tree a streak of sunlight pierced the winter fog, turning the stucco house next door a garish pink.

21. Julie, 2001

How can I be so scared what someone I don't even know may think of me? She was my mother. Hey, *was!*

No—is.

It feels incredibly too isolated and self-centered, selfish, being so caught up in my own story. Lost in the big white empty room of my head.

Lost in finding the lost.

Silly. I phoned Ma and Daddy this evening again; they wished me good luck, and assured me they support "whatever you do."

I bet.

I have to sleep tonight. Gotta be fresh for her.

It's like, will I exist if my birthmom won't accept me? Which, clearly, makes no sense.

22. Malca, 2001

"I just had to bring Gabey. No way I could leave him."

"Of course, of course." Malca kept nodding, half-hearing the carousel music through the copse of oak trees, unable to look away from the shining deep eyes, the straight thick hair, the "olive"-dark skin of this daughter and this grandson. Grandson—how could that be? Julie's baby Gabriel was her and Gavin's *grandson*; like the obvious resemblances, the obvious statement glowed around her heart. Julie's long thin fingers, Gabriel's black eyes, the quick way Julie's lips curled when she smiled—each detail was the past in present, like the first view of a newborn. *I am seeing my baby now, and she sees me.*

Malca laughed, joyous with the absurd anachronism.

"This feels weird—strange—absurd. Doesn't it?" Julie's eyes shone. "I *really* love the absurd."

Malca took a long breath. "I feel blessed. My God."

Jeanne smiled. No, *Julie*. It was necessary to accept the name. Then she looked down. "I'm way older than my birthdad, aren't I? When he died."

Time for explanations, then. Malca paused, afraid. "His baby. You were his baby—and our love and the whole fragile world—but also yourself. The most beautiful, vulnerable, wonderful being on Earth. And how could *I* protect you?" She couldn't stop squeezing her hands together. "This was why, Julie. This was why. So your life would stay whole."

The dark eyes brimmed. "Tell me. I want to know."

"Yes." It was necessary. The time had come—the time to explain the whole of it, to describe who they had been, she and Gavin. To tell this woman of this new millennium what those days had been like, and how a worldwide movement first had crested and then been broken—by tanks in Prague, troops in Paris, massacre in Mexico City, police raids and murder in this country. "Some people, like your dad, were framed, to destroy all that they stood for."

Julie's serious expression hid a subtle smile. *At my Sixties rhetoric?* It didn't matter, though; what mattered was that she accept her father's life. That she learn about Gavin, about his dreams, and what he'd sacrificed to help his family—"He took a risk that no one should be forced to"—and about the park and what had happened there. About the blue light and the red-clay gully, and how happy they were later— sometimes—in the mountains. About the footsteps in the forest, men and lights.

She did not tell the girl how Mom, this morning on the phone, had warned, "You know what comes next, you protest this government. I was too young to understand, back in Europe—see how they use their Big Events, these 'leaders.' Be careful, please—you warn my granddaughter. Take care of Jay, take care of Marvy, for me. Please. Remember what happened." It had been a hard conversation; Mom found everything difficult, these two years, without Dad.

Now Julie was saying, "I thought my birthfather—I always thought he must have been an Indian or Arab or, well, something. With my looks, I mean. I don't know why I thought my Jewish part was you—I mean, 'her'—I mean, my first mother." Julie laughed, and reached over to bring out pictures from her woven Guatemalan bag. There were nearly twenty photos. They showed her at six years old with her white dog Shadow and Silvertip the tomcat, and at sixteen with Mina and Rachel, her friends from high school, and with the whitehaired man and woman, blond and brunette in the earliest photos, who were her Ma and Daddy. A picture of her wedding to Bill, under an actual *chuppah*, and three Polaroids that Bill had taken of baby Gabriel—coming out of the birth canal, lying on Julie's stomach with the cord attached, and, a bit later, nursing.

"This is the world," Malca said.

The younger woman dipped her head and, as if in decision, leaned her forehead against Malca's shoulder. "Hey."

Malca patted the silky hair, not wanting to stop. *Gavin, if only you could be here.*

"Mom-mee, Mom-mee!" Arms raised, Gabriel was running toward them, fleece jacket blotched from rolling down the lawn. Then his smile collapsed and he flopped forward, pulling on his mother's sleeve. He looked into her face. "You sick, Mom-mee?"

"Oh no." Julie sat straight; she patted the short green bench. "Come here, Gabey. I'm just glad to see Granma Bernovski again."

"Granma? Not Granma." He was pulling himself up on his mother's lap; her arms enclosed him. Peeking across them, he stared at Malca, peering from her hairline to her eyes, from the lines by her mouth to the scarf around her neck. "New Granma?"

"I told you, today we see Granma Bernovski. Other-other granma."

Like Granma and Grandpa Bernovski—the 'other' grandparents, Dad's parents with their big country mansion in Tennessee. And clout enough, she still remembered with the half-stifled gratitude, to have kept her from being sentenced even to community service.

"Granma Boofski," Gabriel said agreeably. His face was thin for a preschooler's, and his dark eyes kept glancing for response, *Look, look at me.*

Malca, it's a blackbird. Look. The woman cop had ordered *Don't look—sit down there on that bench,* but the words had been background, the universe locked inside the green bag swung, forever in the iron-hard cold, into the metal blackness.

"Malca? I mean Mother—"

"Just glad you're here. Doing fine, just glad you're here." Here in this unexpected vulnerability. Here in this intensity of love where they each could wield a deadly hurt but were instead—like mother and newborn, new lovers, souls re-met in paradise—protective, caring. Again, she squeezed her daughter's hand.

"Malca, where are you?"

"Other-where." It was her name for that real world, the name she told no one. "When we lived, your father and I. The world that was his, too."

"*Other-where?* But that's where we"—Julie's eyes widened—"we adoptees, you know—where we say our first parents live. Other-where— where we too live, in a way. Oh, this is so weird."

A few clouds had moved in overhead. A longhaired man, possibly a college student, hurtled down the path, riding an old blue mountain bike.

"I should've brought Gabey's tricycle. Sometimes he'll ride all afternoon. Or he builds forts. Or plays chess. His version." Julie grinned. "Hey, you know, where your knights knock the kings off the board."

Malca tried to grin back. Now she knew to whom the set of ancient twigs and tiny stones would someday go.

Julie was reopening her bag, pulling out books—*The Pokey Little Puppy, Over in the Meadow,* and *The Engine that Raced the Moon.*

"Read. Read, Mom."

"No, I don't think so, Gabey. You read. Read for five minutes, okay? And then you get to show Granma Bernovski. She's never heard you read."

He had taken a book and fingered a page, as if about to tear it out. "No."

"Yes. Gabey, you read, go on. I mean it. Read to where the engine gets to Jupiter and back. And after *that,* you can read to Granma, and, after *that,* I'll read awhile."

"Why?" But his eyes were scanning the type. "Boofski Boofski," he repeated, "Boofski," and then his rhythm changed, his words becoming singsong, "So the two brave engines raced up, up, up *up* the mountain, and then green engine steamed far, *far* ahead, out where the ashterode-in-chief was rolling, rolling . . ."

"Julie, you're doing a brilliant job."

"Let's give Gabey some credit." The young woman's smile was like her father's, head slightly bent. After a moment, she tossed her hair. "Gabey's too sensitive, you know? I know it's good, sensitivity and all—hey, really—but . . . Like last night."

"What happened?"

"Oh . . . Well, oh. Oh well, I think it was just the news—the television."

"My dear, half of us on this planet have been . . . oversensitized since September. I mean, to news."

Julie's eyes shone wet beneath her straight brows. "They showed some children who'd been bombed. Maybe Afghanistan? Wherever—I could not take him into daycare today. The place was open—that's not it; Matilda doesn't close. She says, 'I keep open for mommies who work, holidays and any days.' And they're just wonderful with Gabey, she and Annabelle. With all the kids. But after last night—no. He was way too upset. And maybe I was."

A frightened smile crossed Julie's face. "So, after the news, Bill put Gabey down to bed—it was already late—and then he read to him, and then I did, and I sang. Gabey just loves it when I make him songs. But, three hours later, we were fast asleep and all at once there's this noise from Gabey's room. Strange noise, actually—his window squinching open." She dabbed at her eyes. "Bill told me, later, he'd been reading Gabey the one about Santa making elves, and maybe that's what did it, but . . . Anyhow, so we went racing down that hall so fast, and there he was, somehow Gabey'd shoved the window open—I don't know how, it's heavy—and he was climbing out onto the ledge. And he looks at us from there, he's way outside and he's pleading, 'Mommy-Mommy, Daddy-Daddy, help me—someone's fa'wing sideways. Sideways, Mommy—help.' As if it were he who had to stop somebody's fall."

"A nightmare—Julie, he was having a nightmare. Nothing to—"

But Julie was bent over, laughing hysterically, "Hey, gonna be all right."

"Julie-Jeanne." Malca hugged her. "I never didn't love you."

Of course the boy was sensitive. And now he was running toward them. They both leaned forward, stretching out their arms to help him climb up to the bench. For several minutes, they sat still; Gabriel kept smiling as if satiated with content.

"I hope." Julie paused. "I just really hope he gets to g-r-o-w u-p. You know? I mean, all these threats and now they're saying let's go—." She stopped herself. "Oh, you know what I mean, more w-a-r. Oh damn, can't even talk! But you know what I mean, right? Who is it wants that stuff? If those guys keep on—"

Malca squeezed her daughter's hand. "So we try to stop it. For the children. For him."

Gabey yawned, curling into his mother's lap. Black hair shaded his eyes; he held the *Engine* book and his green tyrannosaurus.

Oh, Gavin, you created this. You and I, love.

And so how could it have happened, how could it occur, that only the living—they here, so full of sorrow and joy in this time and place, and only they—were here now, and so blessed? How could it be that none of this could matter, could even *be*, for those who already lay beneath the ground, and had not lived into this day?

"Look. Sq'rrl." Gabey pointed. "'Mazing sq'rrl. See?" Julie's head turned, dark-browed, proud in profile, following his gaze.

But the creature scrabbled, in a scuttle of falling bark and yellow teeth, up the spruce beside them. Malca's arms reached out, an automatic gesture, between that feral hunger and the child. The wild hard eyes stared back, in fury or in terror, the animal rushing upward only to scurry down and then return. It too must have a family to protect. As Gavin had forever lifted up and reached back down to save his people, to save her, that family, that lost world.

Family. For an instant, it was as if Jeff stood beside her, gleaming like the knight he'd first appeared, long lips saying "Love, I'll always shield you, I shall build a firm reality," hard-muscled hiker's body closing toward her own. In his outstretched right hand was a book and in his left a sword, and his voice went deep to set her free of every trap he saw in wait. But his "Choose," all that—they made no sense, those flash-pan ultimatums. Unless indeed he'd meant them. No matter—whatever that led to was no part of today. Being whole meant being here—for both her families, for all her family.

She spread out her arms and lifted them above this little boy, this daughter. *So much love. We are people holding hands, like those in that blue-lit New York morning, clasping while we tumble down—and this is all.* Seeking to protect, whether by holding close or by letting go.

But never again would she let go this child. And to let go Gavin was not possible; to let go Gavin would mean to give up all that they had known, the truth and hope there once had been and now must be again. For the terror in New York that September, the vengeful terror unleashed since, were indeed the old horror returned, and to try to end that nightmare, to help Gabey grow up unscathed and in peace, she too must, once more, embrace the world—yet embrace it without loss of that other core of empathy, without turning the dead into mere memory or stepping forward across their graves. For it was only by carrying the dead, upholding their dream as if to finally breach time's wall—it was only by reaching past the possible, seeking to save everyone, to bring life *through* the darkness—that any of it could make sense and those now living go on. Only by not denying Gavin could she choose life. And indeed, to give Gavin up would mean to give up all of life and love—to give over to death all reality.

23. Malca, 2008

*A*s if the survivor were noble. *As if there is any point, to we who lie beneath the earth.* But it was not this thought had wakened her, or the answering nearly automatic words, *Kaddish, the prayer for the dead, offers praise and gives thanks for our blessings.*

She listened, lying still. Breath slow and sated, exhausted from arguing this week's cases for "illegal" immigrants against the ICE, Jeff slept beside her—beloved Jeff, his fears and ultimatums of the years before bare memory. Jason, home for a month of research and pre-Thanksgiving dinner before he headed east again to start his thesis, and Marvin, sated from a camping trip in the North Cascades, were not yet stirring. Mama-Deluxe, the orange-and-white cat from the Berkeley Humane Society, lay curled, tail over nose, on the walnut hutch. All around, the walls stood, seeming firm—the house walls, and those others.

It had been so long since time was breached. She could *remember* Gavin, these days. Much as she *remembered* the birth of their daughter, now a straightforward, still young-looking mother of a second child, bearing Gavin's life's blood through this world though he was gone. And of course this burdened mother was busy—two children, one still a toddler, plus a demanding faculty job. Yet once it had seemed, in their reunion's overwhelming love, that they were forever close-rejoined. Only, "My parents feel no need to meet my birthmother," Julie had explained, just before that first Mother's Day, and added, "Please don't come over this weekend. Mamma and Daddy will be visiting."

Malca watched the fading stars out the window. After all, it was those parents who had raised her daughter, who . . . etcetera; she had long been tired of going over it all. For her daughter, those people were Mom and Dad; this was set firm as in stone. Besides, everyone complained of not seeing their kids enough. Or else too much. She was fortunate; so far, Marvin came home for only a comfortable proportion of vacations, and Jason hadn't yet become totally caught up in his dissertation. Last New Year's—well, the day after—both the boys had danced around the living room with laughing Gabey to a sarabande from *Terpsichore* and then to "Mom's old music"—meaning "Sound of Silence"—while, standing in a doorway cradling newborn Jennie, Julie watched and rocked from foot to foot.

Even years back, really, on that first afternoon hugging her daughter and Gabey, she had understood: whatever Jeff decided, it was more than enough that she had this child and grandchild and the boys. Gavin had died very early; he had missed so much, missed all these years, *all this*. As she would miss the years of serious Gabey's and elegant Jennie's adulthood. As the people in those falling towers of 2001 had missed their future, as the people had in Baghdad, in Afghanistan, in . . . in wherever came next, and the homeless couple found in January frozen on a bench in Union Square, the brilliant woman dying downtown in a hospital right now. At least, Gavin had died quickly, and for someone he loved.

Every one so soon dead in this count. Each year turning under. No reason—no sense to it, ever. Yet life, love, blessings. Seven years now since the hole had opened in the great impenetrability of time.

And tonight—last night, rather, with Julie phoning, "Turn on your TV, he's won, Obama's won," and Jason emailing a clip from San Francisco, people dancing in the streets, and Marvy so excited, only shrugging when she warned "We'll see" and "He's no radical." Here too on the quiet streets, the cheering voices had leapt, and carried her and Jeff outside to join the singers, arms linked, Jeff's blue eyes alight and she with wide smile pasted on.

Who had written those famous lines, "To be alive then was pure bliss"? But it wasn't so simple, was too forced and false a hope.

Malca turned, making sure the striped sheet and fleece blanket stayed tucked around her husband's shoulders. She wanted no false reassurance from him now, however well intended, but sometime this morning she must say it, "The doctor phoned back yesterday, Jeff. Some tiny nodules showed up in my scan." Really, the dream that woke her had felt startled, angry at the injustice of her dumb philosophy professor saying no he could not pass her if her sewing course were not complete, though she had finally explained she was about to graduate and the sewing class a joke, beneath her, grades just numbers, and besides she had no way to match that shade of leaf-green cloth with some other "what do you call it, 'lot'?" Until finally he said he would accept the off shade, but only if she finished; but this meant her future could not be at all as she had planned.

A bargaining dream, she supposed, expressing an unacknowledged anger—*an anger I must tap? Why do I dread that?*—and hopelessness, despair at the ridiculous, stupid, absurd unfairness. This was only the beginning, probably, beginning of the end of everything. And when the path into that end turned horror, would she dare (as then she must) to *not* choose life? Feeling the air slip in and out her nostrils, beginning to sense how hard it might be to let go, she understood, with startled awe, what Gavin once had given with those pills. Malca lifted her hand from the fleece, careful not to wake the man beside her, and watched the wide half-curtained window while she listened to the frightening, beautiful arrival of the dawn.

Reader's Guide

Interviewer: Reviewers have asked how a sheltered and fastidious young woman like Malca finds the courage and will to approach, touch, and even clean and hold a filthy, probably dangerous stranger in the woods. Does her decision spring, at base, from her legacy of family tales of Holocaust rescue?

Paula Friedman: Certainly family memories are involved. Yet all we really know is that Malca, though very frightened, responds empathetically to this suffering human being by stepping forward, despite all words of caution, to help. Michelle Cliff has called this "characterization." Later, Gavin tells Malca how much he admired her response: "You were scared, but you kept coming closer."

Interviewer: Speaking of the Holocaust, what Malca's mother experienced in Poland essentially parallels what Gavin's father suffered in Syria. Yet Beyla Bernovski, Malca's mother, glows with strength, while Gavin's "Papa" is crushed into passivity. Is this an innate difference in character?

Paula Friedman: Fortunately, the nature-nurture controversy will continue without help from today's fiction writers. This is not a question this tale concerns.

Interviewer: You call Gavin a "complex character," and certainly his viewpoint swerves—even alarmingly—from tough cheerfulness to self-condemnatory despair, from brilliant musicality to something like clinical obsession. Is Malca right when she fears him?

Paula Friedman: We don't know until she finds out. Balancing this uncertainly was, in fact, the hardest part in doing this book—that, and writing Gavin. Like, is this guy Raskolnikov or another OCDC Hamlet? The other difficulty was bringing in nonviolence without proselytizing.

Interviewer: And the matter of Arabs and Jews, of course—obviously a major subtext. Was it planned?

Paula Friedman: When I began the book, the war in Afghanistan was already raging, and Middle Eastern people were anathematized. I'd had close Arab friends in France, and the demonizing of Muslims after 9-11 felt like a personal threat—especially with antiwar activists, too, being attacked. When one irate "patriot" knocked me to the ground at a demonstration, I determined that my writing, too, must stand against injustice.

Interviewer: Yet, in essence, *The Rescuer's Path* is a love story?

Paula Friedman: Every uncertainty that Malca feels about Gavin, every fear for Malca and each self-doubt that Gavin knows, comes not only from their desperate situation but also from the hesitances universal to new, adoring love. Later—both in her marriage and when, eventually, her grown-up birth child finds her—Malca again experiences this love.

Interviewer: As you know, the latter theme—specifically, the adoption reunion—has been criticized as distinct from the major issues of the novel's earlier, "1971" portions. Yet to you these are linked?

Paula Friedman: Oh yes. Malca can never heal completely from the tragedy of 1971. But this birth child connects those lost weeks with the future—indeed, reopens a future.

Interviewer: As, indeed, time figures intensively within the book's structure. On their last evening together, the lovers watch a sunset and Malca envisions the clouds as the gates opening for the Jewish New Year, the eight days when God decides who is to live and who to die.

Paula Friedman: And when those eight days end, on Yom Kippur, the day of atonement—of at-one-ment—God has decided and the gates are closed.

Interviewer: When Malca confronts her own mortality, however, the situation is more mundane.

Paula Friedman: Yet she again reaches out, pulling a blanket over her husband's shoulders as once she had simply aided the shivering fugitive. Only now, sensing how hard death may be, she sees how great had been Gavin's gift.

Interviewer: So is *The Rescuer's Path* primarily political or primarily about life?

Paula Friedman: I see the novel primarily as a story of Malca and Gavin and their child in a particular time.

About the Author

Paula Friedman's honors include Pushcart Prize nominations and OSPA, New Millennium Writings, and other awards and honors, as well as Centrum and Soapstone residencies and fellowships. Her short fiction and poetry have appeared in numerous print and online literary magazines and anthologies. Her books include the novel *The Rescuer's Path* (Plain View Press, 2012, 2018), her novel *The Change Chronicles* (Lillicat Publishers, 2018) and a poetry chapbook, *Time and Other Details* (Highlights Press, 2006).

Ms. Friedman is an author and freelance book editor residing near Portland, Oregon. She has previously taught writing workshops in Hood River, Oregon, directed public relations for the Judah Magnes Museum in Berkeley, California, directed the international Rosenberg Award for Poems on the Jewish Experience, and founded the collective literary magazine *The Open Cell*. She has run poetry readings and writers workshops in the Bay Area, Paris, and elsewhere, and recently compiled an anthology of West Coast Jewish women's poetry. She holds an M.A. from San Francisco State University and a B.A. from Cornell University. A reunited birthmother and former welfare mother, she is active in peace and social justice issues and received the 2006 award of the Columbia River Fellowship for Peace.